THE BUGLES OF GETTYSBURG

"Listen! Again the shrill-lipped bugles blow"

THOMAS BAILEY ALDRICH

(*Sonnet "Gettysburg"*)

"All these the echoing bugle brings again"

FRANCIS F. BROWNE

(*Sonnet "Bugle Echoes"*)

"LEADING his men into the flames of battle with a chivalrous lightness and grace." [Page 120]

THE BUGLES OF GETTYSBURG

BY

LASALLE CORBELL PICKETT

(MRS. GENERAL GEORGE E. PICKETT)

AUTHOR OF "PICKETT AND HIS MEN" "LITERARY HEARTHSTONES OF DIXIE," "IN DE MIZ SERIES," ETC.

SECOND EDITION

CHICAGO

F. G. BROWNE & CO.

1913

PUBLISHED, MAY, 1913

SECOND EDITION, MAY, 1913

THE · PLIMPTON · PRESS
NORWOOD · MASS · U · S · A

AS I SIT ALONE IN THE TWILIGHT SHADOWS THE VISIONS OF
THE MORNING COME BACK TO ME RADIANT WITH FAITH
AND HOPE AND LOVE, EVEN THOUGH DARKENED SOME-
TIMES BY CLOUDS OF WAR. FROM THE MEMORY-
FABRIC MADE OF ALL THOSE GOLDEN DREAMS
THAT CENTER AROUND MY FIRST SOLDIER
I TAKE THE THREADS TO WEAVE THIS
LITTLE STORY OF OLDEN DAYS,
LOVINGLY DEDICATED TO
HIS NAMESAKE SON,

MAJOR GEORGE E. PICKETT, U. S. ARMY

MY LAST
SOLDIER, WHOSE
LIFE LINKED THOSE
VIVID DAYS WITH THE PRES-
ENT, AND WHO CAME HOME ACROSS
THE SEA FROM THE FAR-OFF PHILIP-
PINES WITH EYES CLOSED TO EARTH TO BE
FOREVER OPENED TO THE LIGHT OF ETERNAL DAY

CONTENTS

THE BUGLES OF GETTYSBURG

July 1–3, 1863

The Bugles of Gettysburg

PROLOGUE

ASHES OF GLORY

HALF a century has passed since the Bugles of Gettysburg first echoed from height to height, over hill and valley, the thunder of the red artillery, the rush of the charging cavalry, the tread of the advancing infantry, reverberating with unremitting roll of musketry over the field furrowed and torn by shot and shell, watered and stained by the life-blood of friend and foe alike.

Today the bugles of Gettysburg are heard again, not by armed men with surging passions, putting a question of empire to the arbitrament of the sword, but a quiet throng with the gentlest phases of their nature awakened to sad and awesome memories of those battle days in which a Nation was saved and a Nation was lost.

Three persons are standing in the valley looking in awed silence at Seminary Ridge and across the sunlit space to the range opposite, as if the long ranks of men who passed over that ground fifty years ago were before their eyes and they heard the crash of the guns that made deadly gaps in the line.

One of them is an old man, white-haired and stooped, with a step that has lost its youthful alertness. He is in the darkening shadows of life's dimming twilight and yet as he wanders over the historic field the bugles of the past echo in his heart and his pulses bound again with the fervor of youth. The winds of battle sweep around him as he follows the flag up that flame-crested height to the mouth of the blazing guns.

Beside him is a gentle-faced woman with a wealth of gray hair in soft waves around her face, and dark eyes that hold sad memories of one who lost his life there. Her gaze is lifted above the old line of march, seeking visions beyond the mountains. An officer in the blue uniform of the United States Army looks down at her with filial love.

"I was thinking, my son, of him whose name you bear, my Cousin Garnett," she said in a tone that dwelt lingeringly upon the name she loved. The Colonel pressed her hand tenderly. He was one of the first to answer President McKinley's call for volunteers. Side by side with his father who, Confederate veteran as he was, had volunteered with him and donned the Federal blue at his country's need, he served through the Spanish War, and was commissioned in the regular army. Now he heard wonderingly the echo of the bugle notes of those olden days and looked hopefully into the future, dreaming that it might hold for him the glory, even though it threw over him the gloom, of those fame-crowned hills.

Reminiscences of the day that seemed to belong to a lost age came surging back to the older man.

"Here, Garnett, my son, is where we marched through the fires of destruction up, — yes, up to the very gates of hell. It was terrible — terrible — 'magnificent, but not war' — no, not war — not war."

The woman clung shudderingly to his arm and looked up into his face, whispering, "And where — where —?"

"Over there, I think, my dear, over there," he replied in a tone dropped low in tenderness, gazing toward the outer edge of the field. "Yes, somewhere over there, my son, is the grave of my comrade to whom I owe life and you and all that is good."

"How much the old heartsome word, comrade, means, Aylett, as you say it today!" murmured the woman.

The younger man stood silent, looking questioningly at them both and then across the field, marveling over the vision his father called up of half a century gone.

"Yes, my son, the God of Battles, who holds the universe in the hollow of his hand, knew that the safety of the Union was the safety of the States, and He willed that they should be brought back, each for each."

The echoes of the bugles of Gettysburg will forever carry around the world the fame of Lee and of Meade, of Longstreet and Pickett and Hancock, Hill, Pettigrew, Birney, Slocum, Kemper, and Trimble. They tell us anew of the daring deeds of the Philadelphia Brigade. They sound "taps" over the unknown grave of Garnett sleeping where he fell. They sound a pæan for Fauquier's son, Armistead, and echo his last words as, with cap on sword, he led his brigade up to the Federal guns, calling out:

"Remember, boys, remember! Follow me! Strike for your homes, your wives and your sweethearts! Come, follow me!"

They thrill with memories of the brave men of his brigade, of his Colonels, Hodges, Magruder, Edwards, Griggs, all of whom were killed, and of his Lieutenant-Colonels, Phillips, White, Aylett, all wounded; of Colonel Charles Peyton, the leader of the Game-Cock Regiment, going into battle with the one arm left to him from an early battle; of Williams, Mayo, Patton, and Otey.

Yes, the bugles will ever tell of Dearing and Caskie, of Clopton and Cushing and Stribling and Cowan, and the many who bore well their part here in those fiery days, to meet no more till they had passed into the Mystic Land.

With those names that are emblazoned upon the page of history go the spirit and the force and the courage of the thousands of nameless heroes who reached the last great height of sacrifice and left the memory of the private soldier as a priceless legacy to their country.

The bugles of Gettysburg bear a message of peace today — the peace which the battle fore-

CHAPTER I

SOLDIERS OF VIRGINIA

"THE latest news is that Virginia has seceded."

"Yes. I wonder what the Captain will do."

The young Lieutenant sitting just within the door raised his head as the speakers passed. The lines of his mouth drew tense and his brown eyes deepened almost to black.

"Whatever the Captain may do, there is only one thing the Lieutenant can do," he said to himself grimly; "only one thing, and it is like letting out the heart's blood to do it."

The one thing that the Lieutenant could do must be done at once. The first mail east must carry his resignation to the War Department. But at what cost, at what terrific cost!

He sat long in the dusk, gazing out upon the flag floating proudly from its staff. The waving of its red, white, and blue folds thrilled him as in the olden times. He could not recall a day when that banner had not been to him a sacred thing. There came memories of boyhood days in his home city when he watched it fluttering in the wind, borne at the head of a long line of veterans of 1812, celebrating the triumphs they had won in their hot-blooded youth. He remembered the ambition that filled his heart as he thought that some day he too would be one of a long blue line to celebrate hard-won battles.

The old time at West Point, its hardships and ambitions, its work and fun, its boyish dreams; they all came back now that the old life was done.

And over them all the old flag had waved.

Before his heart's vision waved another flag, deep blue, bearing the legend "Sic Semper Tyrannis," the motto of Virginia, Mother of States, Mother of Presidents, and, nearer and dearer to him, Mother of his home and of all most loved by him.

Over mountain and plain, across desert and forest, came that loved and loving voice: "Come back to Virginia. Come home! Come home!"

"Come back to Virginia." He would answer the call through all the long and weary miles choose; but Virginia, the State that gave me birth, and my father and grandfather before me — she needs me, she calls me —"

He took a step forward as if he saw a vision. His voice broke and sank almost to a whisper.

"She calls me — and — I cannot choose — but — go."

He stepped back and steadied himself against a chair.

"Forgive me, Captain." He bowed. "I beg your pardon."

"Be seated, Lieutenant."

There was no change in the level tone, but the Captain's face was white.

"Be seated, please." And after a moment, "Have you anything further to say?"

"Only this, Captain Pickett. I should like to add that, as it has been no small part of my happiness in the Army to be under your command, so the leaving of that command is no small part of my unhappiness in withdrawing from the Army. I have been proud, very proud, of my Captain. I am sorry, more than sorry, to go."

Again he bowed with military formality.

"And now I must not detain you longer. I should not have come at such an hour."

He awaited permission to retire, but it did not come.

"There is no haste, Lieutenant. There is still time before dinner."

The Captain spoke absently, and toyed with an Indian knife lying on his desk for use as a paper-cutter. Then he rose and began to pace back and forth in the restricted space between the walls.

"You know, of course, Lieutenant, that I also am a Virginian?"

"Yes, Captain."

"Did you suppose — did you think that I should not be tempted? That it would be no struggle for me to remain with the flag we have served together so long?"

His head was bent and Jasper could not see his face.

"I could not judge for any but myself, Captain," he said at length. "In other circumstances I should have come to you and consulted you and been guided by the course you took. But — I have a mother and sister in Virginia; they and the old home must be guarded. And — I have a sweetheart. The woman who is to be my wife has no brother to fight for her. There are many reasons why I should return when my State calls me."

Captain Pickett, still pacing slowly back and forth, hands behind him, paused before the Lieutenant and raised his head.

"Lieutenant Carrington," he said, "I, too, have battled with myself, have felt my heart-strings strained to breaking point as I thought of the old flag, have heard Virginia calling, calling." He put his two hands on the Lieutenant's shoulders. "And I, too, cannot choose — but — go."

They stood thus, gazing into one another's eyes. Then Lieutenant Carrington's fell.

"Bravo, my Captain!" he whispered.

The Captain turned slowly to his desk and laid his hands heavily on a large official envelope.

"I sealed this a few moments before you came," he said in a low tone. "It contains my resignation from the United States Army. God forgive me, but it must be so."

He held out his hand and the two soldiers who had sacrificed so much clasped hands.

"Now," said the Captain, "we are no longer officers of the United States Army; we are soldiers of Virginia with no formalities of rank between us, one in devotion to her service."

After the Lieutenant had gone the Captain stood long in sad meditation, not like one who hesitates, but as a man who takes leave of all his past life.

He thought of the man who had first made the aspiration of his youth the realization of his manhood. A heavy sadness came with the memory. How that dear old friend — now the head of the Nation, the man at the wheel of the Ship of State — would grieve when he knew that at the parting of the ways his cadet had taken the opposite road.

He recalled his first experience of the realities of war — the war with Mexico which had first shaken his youthful conviction that his country could not even by a hair's-breadth be anything but right. The memory of those early days of battle returned through the years; the wearisome march over sun-baked roads under tropical skies, the rush up embattled heights to flaming summits.

Then came the campaigns of the wind-swept plains; the sharp, swift conflict, the triumph, and then — the part that he loved — the uplifting of the conquered to a higher life, a knowledge of the ways of peace, of something better than ghost dances and the slaying of enemies. Whatever might come to him in after life, he should remember with joy that he had brought some of the light of knowledge into the lives of the children of the plains.

And the flag waved over it all! Always the flag! Always its blue sky with the fixed stars shining down and its red and white folds waving in the breeze! Always the flag, beckoning, leading on to victory. Always the flag — the flag!

CHAPTER II

THE VOYAGERS

THE winds were whirling the dust of San Francisco into the face of a man who had just landed from a south-bound steamer and was walking up Clay Street from the rickety old wharf. His hat was pulled low upon his forehead, his gray tiger-eyes almost hidden by its brim. He was opposing a strong front against the wind, like one used to battle.

So absorbed was he in the conflict and so blinded by the dust that he did not see a fellow-sufferer coming in the opposite direction until made aware of him by a sudden impact which thrust them both into the friendly shelter of an overarching entrance, where they looked at each other breathlessly.

"Carrington!" cried he of the tiger-eyes. "Is it possible? How very remarkable, after missing our rendezvous."

They clasped hands in a way that signified not only old-time friendship but a new-born tie so strong that it needed not words to attest its fidelity.

"It is indeed remarkable, Captain. I've been wondering how on earth we should find each other."

"Yes. I wasn't able to leave the post five days after you as I planned, and through that I missed a boat. I've only just got in. I was going to hunt for you, but had no idea where to begin."

The wind swept around the corner and scudded off with the Captain's hat, which his companion caught and restored to its owner. Then with a start of surprise he said:

"It is you, Captain, all right, but — Narcissus without his tresses, Apollo without his lute." Laughingly he went on, "What on earth did you do it for? How did it happen?"

"I didn't 'do it for.' It was an accident."

"An accident? You don't say so."

"Yes. Just before I left the post I went into the shop to have my hair trimmed as usual, and it seems the barber was a new man. He says he asked me about it and I said yes, or murmured something he took to be yes. I was, naturally, very much absorbed in thought, and perhaps I did. Anyway, I noticed nothing till my locks lay on the floor. But I've realized since that it was a good thing. Perhaps it wouldn't be safe for me to be standing talking to you here, otherwise."

"I suppose not. And we must get away as soon as possible. But don't worry, Captain. Your own mother wouldn't recognize you when you're not speaking. I knew your voice, but if I had seen you before you spoke I never in the world should have suspected that it was you."

"This blustering wind has its compensations, then. It has saved us our search for one another. But you, Carrington?"

"Oh, I'm safe enough. As you see, I'm roughing it, and nobody but a faithful friend with eyes and heart like yours would know me. Come, let's go over to Peter Job's."

"Peter Job's? That sounds rather too apostolic and redundant of virtue for a pair of rough soldiers."

"It is appetizing and redundant of hospitality, at any rate, and we can get a spread and a bottle of good Heidsieck, and lave our souls in golden memories before the overshadowing events become too heavy to be forgotten."

Into the driving wind they went again, crossing to Washington Street and passing the Opera House to Peter Job's, where they secured a table in an alcove hidden by a curtain. It was the leisure time between luncheon and dinner and most of the tables were deserted. Later two men in the uniform of the United States Army came in and took seats at a table near them, looking carefully around the room and afterward bending their heads together over a piece of paper.

"Medium size; good build; graceful form; long, curling brown hair; gray eyes with shades of blue; fair complexion; picturesque appearance," one of them drawled after draining his third glass.

"Hair is always uncertain. It might be cut."

"Eyes ought to have a permanent significance, but if sometimes blue and sometimes gray how the dickens can you tell?"

"Fair complexion; all right unless he paints."

"Picturesque; probably he does."

Carrington, hidden behind the curtain, exchanged glances with his companion and anxiously waited till their neighbors were gone.

As they went down the street they saw the

two officers opposite. At the corner the Captain and Jasper turned down a cross street. The blue-uniformed men followed, as if they too might have been incidentally going in that direction. When they reached the next corner the Virginians turned again and looked. The officers still followed them.

At the next turning were two men fighting, a group of street idlers blocking the way. Skilfully eluding the pack, the Captain and Jasper had the satisfaction on looking back of seeing the unknown officers caught in the mob and jostled to the pavement. While the victims were extricating themselves Jasper drew his companion down a flight of steps into a subterranean apartment. The room was empty, and Jasper hurried through it, holding the Captain by the hand. They passed through the door on the opposite side and came into the open street, where they called a hack. Giving an order to the driver they speeded up the street. They did not see a dark man of sinister aspect who looked in vain for another vehicle and went his way cursing.

"Neatly done," said the Captain.

"That comes of knowing your San Francisco. I am taking you to my quarters. When you reflect upon the importance of quiet you will understand that they cannot be of a magnificent description, but they will give us a safe shelter. To-morrow the *Uncle Sam* will set sail for New York, and two vagabonds, very much unknown, will be among the passengers. See? I shall reverse the name of our host of this afternoon and become 'Job Peters,' a shipwrecked sailor. And you — you shall be a wandering troubadour from Provence and from the twelfth century. You look enough like it, and your guitar will come in place. What name shall you take?"

They talked and planned far into the night, but were up betimes and went early aboard the *Uncle Sam*. They stood together and watched the varied throngs come up the gangplank. Jasper made jesting remarks in an undertone, though Captain Pickett warned him that their conversation must be limited and of the most commonplace character.

"'Yon Cassius hath a lean and hungry look,'" whispered Jasper, as a tall, spare man, his slouch hat low over his eyes and his chin sunk in his collar, passed them with a keen glance. A few feet away the man turned and again looked at them, but Captain Pickett, clever in his part of alien, stared vacantly at him and he went on.

The ship weighed anchor and the long, weary voyage began. She was barely out of sight of land before it began to be whispered about that two of her passengers were of unusual interest even in that motley crowd. One was "Job Peters," a sailor whose graphic yarns enlightened the tedium of the monotonous voyage. The other was "Arnaut Jasmin," from South Europe, a slender, graceful man, having but slight acquaintance with the English language. He would listen to the stories of his sailor companion, now with interest and again with bewilderment as a confusion of new words would interrupt the thread of the narrative. When alone he would take his guitar and sing a sprightly lyric of France or a Spanish serenade, playing an accompaniment as he sang. A group of music lovers would gather round him in moods responsive to the gaiety of his barcarolles or the melancholy of his love songs.

"Lieutenant, have you an enemy?"

The two Virginians stood in a remote part of the boat and trusted themselves to speak naturally.

"I hope so, Captain. I should not like to be so characterless as not to have one."

"But an inveterate enemy, I mean. One who pursues you relentlessly as a supreme object in life, like the villain in the play on the track of the noble hero."

"I have never posed as a noble hero sufficiently to know. Possibly if I should ever distinguish myself in that way such a personality might develop. It would be necessary, as the play could scarcely go on without him."

"I am in dead earnest, Jasper."

"So am I."

"And this may be a tragedy for you. I am trying to warn you."

"Don't do it. Not that I am ungrateful, but you know what the philosophic Arabs say:

"On two days it steads not to run from thy grave —
 On the appointed and the unappointed day;
On the first neither balm nor physician can save,
 Nor thee on the second the universe slay.

"But what on earth has put it into your head just now that I have — what did you call him? — an inveterate enemy? You do not fancy that something is about to happen to me, do you? What shadow do you see upon the deck?"

"It is worse than a shadow; it is a persistent and vindictive looking substance that has caused me anxiety for some days; the spare man with a dark, gloomy, sinister, determined face — 'yon Cassius,' in a word."

"Why, I never saw the fellow before."

"Nor I. But he watches you most malevolently. He may be mad. But I don't like it, and if I were you I'd be on the alert when he's around."

"It must be, then, Captain, that there is some one on board who does not like me. I am grateful to him. You warn me of him? I am even more grateful to you."

"He seems to be one of our own countrymen, strange to say. He speaks most unmistakably the mother-tongue of the blessed State to which we are bound."

"I can't think who he is unless it is that hound Campo. They call him the Raven, because he is dark and gloomy and prophetic of evil. But I beg the raven's pardon; this Raven is more than that: he is thoroughly unprincipled and desperate. I myself don't know him, but have been told that he regards me with especial malevolence because he is jealous. The puppy has the presumption and impudence to imagine himself in love with one whose heart is in my keeping."

"Ah! that sounds reasonable, though not the less detestable. But stay, some one is coming."

And the Captain strummed gently on his guitar and turned a melancholy gaze seaward.

CHAPTER III

SAILORS' REST

WHEN the *Uncle Sam* weighed anchor in New York harbor two of her passengers were standing a little apart from the others, silent amid the commotion of arrival but watching narrowly all that occurred and listening with quiet attention to the conversation that went on around them, their anxiety hidden by an air of casual interest. The dark man they called Cassius stood near them.

When the pilot came on board, the Captain of the ship, with the eagerness of one who has had no word from shore for weeks, called out:

"What's the news?"

"It's a black squall here," was the reply, "and it veers north'ard and south'ard till a man doesn't know which way he's sailing."

"What's the particular blow today?"

"Arrests for treason and all that. One man just brought here in a boat in irons. Let's see — what's his name? He's a Com'dore — Com'dore Barron, — yes, that's it."

"Job Peters" started like one who had received a sudden shock and his friend impulsively moved toward him as if to defend him from a blow. The dark man smiled grimly.

"I can't help feeling that it's kind o' queer to think of Americans being brought to for that sort o' thing, and one with the Com'dore's log-book, too." The ship's Captain spoke irritably. "But I'm not saying anything except it's a time when it pays a man to keep his sails close reefed and hug the shore."

The two quiet travelers had no baggage to detain them, he of the troubadour guise having left all papers and valuables in the care of the British officers who had occupied San Juan with him, and Jasper having abandoned in San Francisco everything that could have betrayed him.

They left the ship separately, meeting a half hour later at a designated point above the wharf, from which they walked on along the water's edge.

"Where are we going, Jasper? New York ought to be big enough to afford us a haven of safety somewhere."

"Yes, but we'll have to be careful where we sail; there are plenty of sand bars on which to wreck our craft and whirlpools enough to sink us to the depths."

"I see you think we are adrift upon an unknown sea."

"Almost, Captain, though I do know one harbor alongshore. It is kept by an old sea captain who is laid up now but never gets far away from the ocean. He must be where he can hear it roll and see it toss up its waves to the sun. He would be lonesome without that, so he stays down here in a place called Sailors' Rest, — he says because sailors have never been known to rest there. He is out of politics, — has never been in. Says he found the water treacherous enough for him."

The silent man knew that his friend was talking against time, talking against thought, talking against feeling. He took his hand and gently spoke his name. The two went on in silence until they reached Sailors' Rest, where they were received by a bluff old seaman, rollicking and jolly, with a walk like the rolling of the waves.

"Jasper Carrington! Many's the storm your uncle, the Commodore, and I have weathered together, and many's the voyage we've taken over waves that rocked as gently as a cradle."

Jasper introduced his companion and the sailor went on:

"You're both as welcome as a sunshiny morning after a squally night; and you, Captain Pickett, — I am as glad to see you as if you had trod the quarterdeck with us."

He led the way upstairs with voluminous expressions of delight. When they were in his loft he shut the door and turned to Jasper with a serious look.

"I know about Uncle," said Jasper. "I heard it as I landed."

"You mustn't cast anchor here very long. There's nothing you can do and you'd only make things worse by getting scuttled yourself. He has shipmates here and they'll do everything that can be done to get him into safe water again."

"I know you will do all that is possible."

"I'll set your sails for a safe harbor where you can look around a bit and get your bearings. Of course, they can't do anything to the Com'dore more'n to keep him in the hold awhile."

"I thought Sailors' Rest was as good a harbor as could be found," said Jasper.

"It looks like it, but loyal as I am and quiet

as I am, they have an eye on my place, for some reason."

A commotion below called the old sailor away and his guests heard him saying:

"On with your serious mug and doctor's coat, shipmate."

He went on down the stairs and his voice came back to them in greeting to apparently unwelcome visitors:

"Officers is it you want? You won't find 'em here. What do you think I want o' shooting irons and cutting things around Sailors' Rest? This is a peaceful harbor for unseaworthy craft to sail into and put up for repairs. You won't find anything here but boats gone to wreck and sea-dogs on their last legs."

"I suppose you will let us look around over your upper deck, will you not? This young man was on the boat with them and heard them arranging to come here."

"There's no one come yet, but go right ahead; no, wait. Better ask old Pill-box first. There's a sick man up there steering straight for t'other world with a gospel pilot towing him in, and you might have to step in quiet. Here comes the medical mate. These gentlemen want to go up, Doc."

"They can't, unless they want to have murder on their souls."

After a moment's consultation they decided to give the sick man his one chance and departed. The sailor returned to his guests.

"I made them believe old Salt-Water Jake was a life-buoy, and he doesn't know a pill from a pulpit. But it's getting rough weather here for you. There's a squall coming up from the north and you'd better up sail and scud before the wind to a safer port."

"None of your ports up this way seem to be very safe," replied Jasper.

"Well, you might have struck a peacefuler landing than this. But there's a gospel tug up in the city hooked to a Ship of Zion away up among the high swells that'll tow you along into smoother sailing and land you on to a shore where the green pastures of peace will lie all around you."

The "gospel tug" mentioned by the old sailor was the pastor of a popular church in New York. Though he was of a Northern family, brother of a man who afterward won distinction in the Federal Army, his sympathies went out to the South. Many a Southron, fleeing homeward to offer his sword to his country, had been protected and helped on his way by the great-hearted preacher.

The two soldiers knew of the minister and his friendship for their cause, and gladly followed the suggestion of their friend.

So often had similar incidents occurred that Dr. Paxton was not surprised that morning to receive a call from the two who were fleeing from the over-warm hospitality of the otherwise frigid North.

"George Pickett and Jasper Carrington, you say? Good names — names that are both dear to me. Nevertheless, I am not sure that I am glad to see you, for the atmosphere here is not very healthful for such as you, my friends."

"Any atmosphere should be healthful where you are, Doctor."

"Ah, if it were," said the minister, "I would diffuse it all over the country and restore sanity and good fellowship."

"You are doing useful work, as it is, in making a haven of restfulness and safety for those who are hastening to the defense of their homes and firesides."

"I do the little that God has given me the power to do. But, come, you have not breakfasted."

"No; our late host, generous as he is, had good reason for not insisting upon our company at breakfast."

"Then you shall give me that pleasure. Breakfast is served and I hope we may be allowed to take it in peace."

But the good man was not permitted to realize his hope. They had just taken places at table when the bell sounded and the host excused himself. Returning he said:

"They have begun early today. It is the third time within a week that my house has been thus honored. Come down this hall and find a hiding-place outside while my faithful butler looks for the door-key which he has accidentally dropped."

He guided them through a hallway into a small garden inclosed by a high wall, beckoning to two men who were fastening to a lattice a rose-vine which had been torn loose by the wind. The workmen came promptly forward, as if accustomed to such interruptions, and put their rough coats and hats upon the newcomers, saying, "Quick, take our places at the roses," and disappeared.

The officers and their sinister-looking guide, having reached the dining-room in their search, looked from the window and saw two men who seemed absorbed in gardening. Raising the window one of them called:

"Have you seen any men going through here this morning?"

"No, sir," said Jasper. "We ain't seed nobody." He spoke with a nasal twang and fumbled clumsily with his hat.

The other workman looked on with an expression of curiosity as if but half comprehending what was said.

Returning to the library the officers took an apologetic leave of Dr. Paxton.

"That is all right, gentlemen," said the Doctor. "These times require strict watchfulness. Good morning."

When the unwelcome callers were gone Dr. Paxton invited the volunteer gardeners to return to their breakfast, at the close of which he said:

"I hope you will not think it inhospitable if I suggest your going at once; it is sometimes far more hospitable to speed the parting guest."

"We thank you, Doctor, with all our hearts for this, the truest hospitality, but the question is, how are we to get away?"

"Remembering a friend is leaving for Canada, I have just sent a message to him hastening his departure by a day or two. His love for me and loyalty to our cause is unquestioned; you will be safe with him."

"Go to Virginia by way of Canada?"

"It is a case in which the longest way around is the shortest way home," he laughed.

That evening George Pickett and Jasper Carrington took the train for Canada, every revolution of the wheels carrying them farther and farther away from the home and friends they were so eager to reach.

CHAPTER IV

CATHERINE

THE dim old library at Magnolia Lawn was very cool and quiet. The sun, which all day had beaten somewhat too warmly down upon the thick vines and closed shutters, now sent his last level rays unhindered through the wide uncurtained windows. One of them, slipping silently inch by inch, at last touched the flowerlike face of a girl sitting in a low chair by the center-table. She glanced at the west windows, then closed the book which had lain idle on her knee. It was useless to try to read; she had not turned a page since first sitting down some twenty minutes before.

She walked slowly to the end of the long room and stood with her hands behind her, looking northward. She did not see the wide gardens nor the fields beyond. She saw, hundreds of miles away, the Northern camp. Floating proudly above it were the once beloved Stars and Stripes. She saw the long ranks of men in blue, and among them, preparing to fight — perhaps already fighting — against his home, his friends, his brothers, was the man she loved. Dear God! could she bear anything so horrible? Surely her heart must break. Surely some terrible illness must smite her, mercifully, to blot out consciousness, memory, torment.

"Why shut up in the library, Cousin Kate? I've been looking for you everywhere."

"Oh, is that you, Garnett?" She turned, with a wan smile, as he crossed the room. "I thought you were busy. I've been trying to read."

"Why 'trying,' if you are not in the mood?"

"Oh, because. It doesn't do to think too much. I can't keep my thoughts from those of our boys who haven't come home yet. Hundreds have come, you know, from all over the country, but there were a good many on the Pacific Coast, and nothing has been heard of them. There is Captain Pickett, for one. It surely cannot be that he would remain with the North. And yet — where is he? No one has heard, no one has any idea. It seems so terrible not to know, doesn't it?"

She was silent for a few moments.

"There are others we know personally. Lieutenant Carrington, of Brightview, the big place over by the gap; I don't believe you've ever met him. The family inherited the place and came there when you were away. His mother and sister are nearly wild. Some one — but an enemy of his — sent word that he was seen in New York days ago, so he must have come east. And his not coming home looks so suspicious. Can you imagine anything that would detain him — that would detain any one after landing?"

"There are always delays, Cousin mine, and of course if our men walked out with French leave — they may not have been allowed to resign, you know — if they deserted, to put it bluntly, they are liable to arrest."

"And what then?" The words were only a whisper.

He glanced at her white, tense face; then closed his big hand over her small one as it hung at her side.

"Nothing, perhaps," he said reassuringly. "A few days' imprisonment, or a mere reprimand, probably."

"You really think so, Cousin Garnett?"

She looked up at him like an eager child.

He turned away his head. He was not used to lying, this clear-eyed young soldier.

"Surely, Cousin mine. But why waste tender sympathy over neighbors and heroes you have hardly seen, when they may not be in need of it? And God knows," he added solemnly, "we may all be in dire need of it before many moons have passed. How doubly, trebly blessed are those of us for whom your special prayers will arise. Ah, Kate, if I might go into battle to-morrow with a word of more than cousinly affection. If you would give me hope, hope. I will wait — for years, if it need be; I won't bother you, if you will only tell me that I carry your love with me when I go. Can you — will you — tell me that? You have had my love so long."

The girl's eyes filled with tears.

"Garnett dear! Dear Garnett! I do love you, but not that way. Please don't be unhappy about it. And you make me unhappy, too. And we should have only sweet, tender memories of your last evening before you go out to fight for us. You go to fight for the South, Garnett, above all, but — you have no sister — when the other men are thinking of their mothers and sisters, if they seem to be fighting for them, I shall be proud—so proud—if you will think of me. We have been more to one another than cousins, Garnett, dear; you have been to me the brother I have never had, and I perhaps to you the sister who died when you were little. You may fight for the South and—and for me, dear Cousin."

She turned to the window, where the twilight was deepening. Her voice sank.

"And each morning and evening, wherever I am, I shall pray for you, that God may bless and keep you and bring you back to us."

He bent and kissed her two hands, reverently.

"It is as God wills," he said gently. "Though I may not have your heart I am more than blessed in having your prayers."

He left the room slowly, as if loth to go.

The girl still stood by the window. He was very dear to her, this soldier cousin. It hurt her to give him pain. She wondered, vaguely, how girls could glory in their conquests when it hurt so much.

She thought of one man whose wooing had frightened her; the only one among many for whom she had felt no pang when she refused him. She had since heard that he had sworn vengeance upon Jasper. What a cowardly — what a despicable — step to take! It was he who had sent word that Jasper had returned to the East but remained in the Union Army.

She lifted a white face.

"Dear God, make it not true! make it not true!"

CHAPTER V

INTO THE HEART OF THE STORM

FROM Canada our travelers rode southward, keeping to trackless wilderness and mountain roads. After some days they struck a narrow pass in the Cumberland Mountains where the range divides the golden fields of old Kentucky from the neighboring lands of Tennessee. A storm had swept down upon the heights and a swirl of strong winds hurled itself wildly over the towering gray ramparts and against the jagged walls of the dark mountain-clefts. Lightnings flashed into the black corridors and thunders reverberated from wall to wall like the crash of guns in a great artillery battle. Riding through the pass the Captain and Jasper stopped under a shelving ledge, sheltering themselves from the blinding sheets of rain.

"I say, Captain."

"Well?"

"This doesn't seem like hospitable Kentucky."

"It does not. When Kentucky was created all the acrid characteristics which might have been scattered through her and injected into the hearts of her people were heaped up along the border line where nobody but outlaws like you and me need ever meet them. Hospitable Kentucky is down there on the level green and gold meadows where the people open houses and hearts to all who come their way."

Jasper looked wistfully down into the valley.

"If the poet expected a cheerful answer to his query, 'What pleasure dwells in heights?' he could not have addressed it to fugitives lost in mountain thunder-storms."

"I have friends down there in the meadow," said the Captain.

"This is the time of need when a friend would be a friend indeed."

A retrospective look overspread the countenance of the Captain.

"The homey enchantment of the old place comes back to me now. The flavor of the wonderful things emerging from that generous larder appeals to me more strongly than did Lucullian banquets to the Roman epicure. And — oh, the bottles of Kentucky sunshine hidden away in the cellar, wound about with spider-webs of decades and crowned with garlands of vanished years!"

"If I ever had a shade of delicacy about accepting unoffered invitations the winds have blown it away. Let's go."

They plunged into the valley, leaping brooks and fences, pounding over rocks and rugged cross-roads and skimming lightly down meadow-paths. The storm followed them, blotting out the stars that flamed in the dusks of the deep sky and filling the night with a cannonade. Entering spacious grounds they cantered up a wide driveway, dismounted and struck the old knocker which had hung upon the front door since "good old colony times when we lived under the king." The door was opened hesitatingly and a face peered out. A gleam of light fell upon the travelers and the door was thrown wide open while a genial voice called:

"George Pickett! I need not tell you how welcome you are."

They entered the wide hall and the Captain introduced his friend. The host cordially grasped the Lieutenant's hand.

"Your friend is necessarily on the right side," he said as he ushered his visitors into a bright room where they were welcomed by a gentle-faced woman.

"I have been watching for your name on our Army list, Captain," said the host, "and have wondered that you were so long delayed. I was half afraid of you when I heard your knock. We have had two visits today; one from cavalrymen who called us rebels and took off our horses, and the other from a detachment of infantry who addressed us as decorated Yankees and killed our cows. You may understand that the experience has tended to narrow our hospitality to strangers."

"It might have that effect."

"Now I shall take you to my room where you will put on what clothes we can find that fit you best and let Mammy Dilsey dry yours by the kitchen fire. After that you are to have an old Kentucky supper such as you have not seen for years. Pomp, bring out the 'Golden Particular'; nothing else will do for an occasion like this."

"Yas, suh," said Pomp from somewhere in the shadows.

If the pleasant home environment and the lulling influence of the Kentucky supper led the travelers to anticipations of a restful night they were doomed to disappointment, as they had not jogged far into Slumber-Land when they were awakened by a vigorous clutch.

"They have come," said the Kentuckian, "and they outnumber us. No, let your pistols alone. You can't afford a fight when you don't know which side the first shot may bring down on you. Come."

The visitors followed him into an unfinished room with unplastered walls and ceiling.

"Up among the joists."

They swung themselves up and, peering down between, waited. Soon afterward footsteps entered the room they had left and came toward their hiding-place. The door opened and Pomp appeared upon the threshold carrying a lighted candle, two officers following him. As the sable guide stepped across the entrance he stumbled and the candle fell from his hand.

"Ef dat can'le ain' done gone en unlit itse'f," grumbled old Pomp from the darkness that followed the accident. "Jes' wait, Marsers, en I'll git a match."

The matches were hard to find and some minutes elapsed before Pomp announced exultantly:

"Hyear dey is. Now we'll hab a light."

There followed a succession of unavailing efforts to strike a light and Pomp's disappointed voice growled:

"'Clar ter gracious! 'pear lak dese matches ain' got no eend 'tall 'cep'n de wrong eend."

After another series of labored efforts he succeeded in lighting his candle and started toward the door where the officers waited. The clatter of galloping horses was heard coming nearer and nearer and then the cry:

"Morgan's Mens! Morgan's Mens!"

"Morgan's Mens is comin'!" shouted old Sambo bursting into the room that was feebly lit by Pomp's struggling candle.

The two officers rushed out of the room, joined their companions who had waited below, and their horses were heard clattering away in the distance. The Captain and Sam leaped from the joists.

"Where are Morgan's Men?"

"De Lawd He know, Marse Cap'n. He's mos' in gen'ally de onlyes' one whut does know. Ober on t'udder side er Ole Kaintuck, I s'pose. Dey wuz hyear yis'day, en any man whut 'spec's Morgan's Men ter be terday whar dey wuz yis'day don' know needer de mens ner needer de hosses."

"But you said they were here."

"Dat's 'cause dey wan't. Ef dey'd been hyear dey'd jes' er crope up silent lak en cotch dem ossifers 'fo' dey'd knowed darse'fs. Jake en Bill jes' got some hosses dat we sont arter, whut de Marser had lef' 'cause we'd rid 'em up de walley a little piece ter de hidin'-place ter sabe 'em fer him, en sot 'em clatterin' down de grabble paf en den we screeched 'Morgan's Mens!' en den you ought ter seed dem blue-coats run."

"I am sorry your rest was disturbed," said their host.

"It's the fortunes of war," replied the Captain.

Next morning the riders were early in the saddle and on a sunny September day the beautiful fields of Virginia spread out before them, barely touched as yet by the fires of war. They circled the Federal lines and on the 12th of September, 1861, they rode into the Queen City of the Confederacy, — into the heart of the storm.

They did not separate until they had been together to the military headquarters and enlisted in the Army of the Confederacy. Then Jasper at once started for home, stopping at Magnolia Lawn as he passed.

It was dusk when he dismounted at the steps and threw the reins to a young negro. The front door stood hospitably wide in the warmth of the early evening.

As he crossed the porch a little figure came running down the long hall and flung itself into his outstretched arms.

"Oh, Jasper, you have come! Thank God, you have come! I was so afraid — they said that you — but you are here, my love, you are here."

She lay sobbing brokenly in his arms.

"Nothing matters — nothing matters — you are here!"

CHAPTER VI

THE AMBER PATH

Sitting by the roadside on a summer day,
Chatting with my messmates, passing time away,
Lying in the shadow underneath the trees,
Goodness, how delicious, eating goober peas.

THE notes of the old song rang out in a fine baritone and wove their way like a silver thread in and out among the leafy branches of a cluster of trees where a group of soldiers were resting after a toilsome march, regaling themselves with the delicacy celebrated in their song, the fruits of a foraging expedition against a neighboring farm where the remains of last year's crop were stored. A chorus of voices, tenor, bass, and nondescript, joined Lieutenant-Colonel Jasper Carrington in the refrain:

Peas! Peas! Peas! Peas! eating goober peas!
Goodness, how delicious, eating goober peas!

They fell to with renewed relish as the echo of their song rolled from tree to tree and out over the river. Jasper finished his repast and lay looking sentimentally through the foliage of the great oak that spread its branches over him, singing with plaintive softness, "Peas! Peas! Peas!" to a gray squirrel peering at him from the crotch of the tree. It scampered off to a very high limb, from which it plucked an acorn and nibbled it, dropping the cup on the upturned face of the recumbent man, who retaliated by throwing the empty shell of the goober toward his saucy enemy.

A strain of music floated through the woodland and Jasper arose and leaned forward in attentive attitude.

"Listen! Hear my old Pete's bugle. Our General is coming. Pete always bugles 'See the conquering hero comes' when he is in sight. Lord! What a world of tones Pete can get out of that old bugle! One might think it a magic bugle. Its plaintiveness almost broke one's heart that day he learned that our General was wounded at Gaines's Mill. Two months later when he came back, though his wound was so far from healed that he could not put on his coat, every note of the bugle was a Resurrection Day note. All the flowers that have ever made the world glad blossomed again. You heard all the birds that had made music in the forest since the first songster trilled his love-song from a branch in the primeval wood. You clasped hands with all the friends whom you had loved in days gone by, and dwelt with all the radiant things that had brightened your life. It was melodized sunlight, love transmuted into music, life triumphant over death."

The tread of a horse was heard in the distance, keeping time to the bugle notes, and soon a powerful war-steed broke through the shrubbery. His rider, a slight, graceful man who sat his horse as if the two were one, was he who on the twelfth of September nearly two years before had enlisted in the Army of the Confederacy and on the following day had been commissioned Captain. Now he was commander of a division of Longstreet's Corps.

His hair, long and curling now, floated in the wind like a cloud-veil. He was not above medium height and the lines of grace he unconsciously followed suggested that his victories in the drawing-room might be no less notable than those he had won on the battlefield. His face was of that fairness which defies the bronzing effect of sun and the darkening shades of time. An expression of deeper thought was the only change that had come to it in nearly two fiery years which had passed since that wild ride from the North into the raging storm.

Born of a race of warriors, schooled in military art, trained in camp and barracks and on the field, a boy soldier in the land of the Montezumas, catching the flag from the hand of his fallen friend, Captain Longstreet, and carrying it to the height of Chapultepec, a determined man, barring with slender force the gate of the West to a foreign foe, he looked not like one to revel in martial deeds, because of the wide and deep and high humanity dominating all smaller attributes as the spirit of God rules supreme over the world.

As he came riding down from the west his form was outlined darkly against the red wine of the sunset that splashed in crimson stains upon an amber-tinted sky.

"The General!" shouted one of the goober pea devotees on the hillside. The cry swept from group to group and the air was rent with cheers. The rider raised his cap and the smile that lit his face brought the rare blue glints to his eyes. Thus he rode till he had passed from view and ringing cheers followed him.

Some distance in advance was a horseman. The General recognized the tall form, the strong, erect shoulders, the soldierly bearing and the superb horsemanship of Lee's "Old War-Horse," whose corps was said by the Federals to be the terror of their army. The younger officer put his horse at speed and was soon beside the tall, handsome Corps Commander.

"How are you, Pickett?" said the Lieutenant-General, laying his hand on the shoulder of his companion.

The two rode on together talking, not as commanding and subordinate officer, but as old friends who had met casually on the road of life.

"You saw her last evening?" asked the older man turning his steel-blue eyes upon his friend, — eyes that were stern and piercing except when the sunniness of his mood made them twinkle with mirth. The sunniness was in them now. "You gave her my message?"

"She sent her thanks and good wishes in reply."

"I am obliged to her. But how do you reconcile it with military tactics to follow Mars and worship at the shrine of Venus both at once?"

"It does not need reconciliation. It is the smile of the gentle goddess that gives us strength to follow the frowning god."

"Suppose Mars should refuse to divide his kingdom?"

"Ah, but he never does. He continues to shed his favors upon you and you have a whole empire of love to claim your devotion."

"But I do not go galloping through forests and over rivers and past hostile sentries of nights just for a look and a word and come dashing back to the field with the first glint of morning."

"A look and a word? But they are worth the hardest ride that ever soldier took."

They rode on in silence for awhile. Then General Longstreet said:

"If we go into the North, — but what do you think of the plan?"

"I think not well of it."

"Nor I. I cannot take the cheerful outlook presented by one of our chaplains, that Providence has at last consented to come down and take a proper view of the situation."

"I like not to strike at other men's homes," said the younger officer. "To defend my own I think my sword would of itself leap out of its scabbard."

His hand went to his side. The Lieutenant-General was filled anew with wonderment that so slight a hand could wield so heavy a sword, but he had seen the flash of that blade in the front of the battle like lightnings in a storm and men rushing after its blaze to the gates of death.

"To choose our ground and let the enemy attack us is the way to win; as at Fredericksburg," said General Longstreet. "There was a battle! I dream nights of the glory of that day, and hear General Lee say, 'It is well that war is so terrible, else we should become too fond of it.'"

"It must have a horrible fascination if it could enchain him, when every man who is killed is a personal loss and sorrow to him. Dear old 'Marse Bob'! What a heart he has!"

Thus Lee's "Old War-Horse" and he who was called the "Bayard of the Confederacy" rode down the amber path of sunset.

CHAPTER VII

UNCLE ZEKE

CATHERINE MARSHALL arose from the chair in the library where she had been pretending to herself that she was reading, went to the window, drew back the heavy curtain and looked out into the night. From a jagged mass of clouds flamed a blaze of lightning which revealed her slim height wrapped in a shroud of fire. A dark form came from a clump of magnolias into the white light.

"Uncle Zeke!" she called.

"Yas'm; dis me, — dis yo' Ung Zeke."

"Come in out of the storm and tell me, quick, please, Uncle Zeke, what you have found out."

Uncle Zeke stepped through the low window into the library.

"I's moughty sorry, li'le Missus, 'boutn what I found out. You know yo' Ung Zeke would gib his ve'y eyeballs fo' you, Honey, but I reckon dey-all's got Marse Jasper dis time fer sho', widout somebody warns him, en dar ain' nobody ter do dat widout we kin fin' a li'le bird roun' 'bout hyer wid moughty spry wings. In de ole times when troubles come dar wuz allus birds ter ca'y orange blossoms in outn de wet en ter ca'y johnny-cakes ter de prophets, but 'pear lak dey's all flewed now."

"What do you mean?" cried the girl. "Please tell me quick what you heard. Oh, Uncle Zeke, are you sure about your Marse Jasper?"

"Is I sho' er jedgment day, Honey? Yas'm, 'co'se I's sho', fer I wuz close 'nough ter de haid debil ter tetch 'im, en yo' Ung Zeke's got moughty good ears. Dey t'inks I's gwine ter run off en leabe you-all en go up yander ter de Norf whar dey-all goes skatin' Fofe-er-July en freezes up ebby Christmas en don' thaw out no mo' 'twel way de naix summer, en whar dey say de lan' is too stiff en hard ter raise we-alls' kin' er perwishuns on, en whar dey nebber hab hot hoe-cakes en beaten biscuits en t'ings, but jes' libs on cole bread."

"But what did they say? Please, — please tell me!"

"Laws a mussy! Hain't I a tellin' you ez fas' ez my ole tongue kin ju'k out de wu'ds? 'Pear lak, Miss Kate, you's in a pow'ful big hurry fer dis time er night. Does you 'spec' my ole tongue ter glib out de wu'ds ez supple ez yourn does? You jes' wait 'twel it's run ez long ez minez."

Catherine clasped her hands pleadingly.

Uncle Zeke fixed his eyes on a flicker of sheet lightning over at the edge of the world and prepared to make the effort of his life.

"Well'm, I got in de room er de Kunnel hisse'f, 'long er my tellin' 'im dat I knowed all 'bout a plan ter grab 'im en all his sogers ez dey come 'long up de road, en how dar wuz a passel er Confedericks absquaterlatin' darse'fs in a clump er underbresh jes' raidy ter jump out at 'em unbeknownst. Hya — hya — I got de Kunnel so tangled up in dat underbresh, Honey, dat he went on axin' queschuns 'twel I mus' a tole, 'im jes' how many bushes dar wuz in it en gin 'im de whar'bouts er ebby briah en blade er grass in de whole road."

"What else, Uncle Zeke? For pity's sake, please tell me what else!"

"Don' you t'ink dat wuz 'nough, Miss Kate? Leas'ways it tuk 'twel all de ossifers wuz a comin' in fer a confabulation 'bout yudder t'ings en I got up ter go. Dat is, dey all thunk I got up ter go, but I didn' hab no such notionment. I jes' went to'des de do' when de ossifers wuz a comin' in en slipped suddent like behime a screen en didn' nobody eben s'picion fer a minute dat I wan't gone. En dat's how I yeard all 'boutn de plan ter ketch Marse Jasper."

Uncle Zeke took a deliberate view of all that could be seen through the darkness and peered out to consider the prospect of clear weather. Catherine breathed a deep sigh.

"Yas'm; don't be onpatient, Honey. Fust off dey talked 'bout some mens up dar in Wash'ton what's gone on a rampage somewhar en won' sen' 'em de t'ings dey-all needs. Den dey talked 'bout Marse Abraham Linkum comin' down ter camp en whut he said. Mebbe you don' keer 'bout whut Marse Linkum said needer, dough, does you?"

"For heaven's sake, no!" groaned Kate.

"Well, den, pres'mly dey 'gun ter talk 'bout Marse Jasper en how dey wuz gwine down to Brightview ter ketch 'im, en how 'at he couldn't git away dis time nohow, lak he did las' time, en how 'at dey wuz gwine ter start a passel er indigo Yanks out atter 'im, en, Honey, I's moughty 'fraid dat it's all up wid Marse Jasper dis time, 'kaze dar ain' nobody ter let 'im know 'cep'n me an' I couldn' git dar in time, ter sabe me, en you, — but den, 'co'se you couldn' go."

"I can go, Uncle Zeke; but you would get there after he was in a Northern prison."

"Mebbe I mought but den I'd show my good will."

"None of us doubts that, my dear old black daddy, but now we want something that will tell in another way. Lightning is the only horse on the plantation that can make the distance to Brightview to-night and you know I am the only one who can ride him."

"Yas'm, li'le Missus, you can ride all right, but you'd be daid ez a do'-nail when you got dar, so it's better fer me ter go, Honey, eben ef I didn' neber git dar."

"No, there is but one way, Uncle Zeke, so, please, sir, go and saddle my dear little horse while I run and get ready."

Uncle Zeke went away grumbling.

"Yas, she's de onlyes' one dat kin ride Lightnin', dat's so, but whut good'll dat do when she's kilt? Ride Lightnin'! I'd lak ter see anybody else ridin' 'im. Didn' fo' er dem Yankee sogers try hit de yudder day en didn' all fo' git flung ober his haid 'fo' dey could say amens? Yas, she kin ride all right. 'Tain't de hoss dat I's skeered er, it's de ride. But nemmine; ole Zeke is gwine wid her en sabe her ef he kin, en ef he cyan't den he kin bring her home daid; dat's all he kin do."

The pet horse whinnied when he heard Kate's voice and rubbed his silvery head against her shoulder.

"I know it's hard to be called away from your dreams, my pretty, but we are going to save life, — his life, Lightning."

"Humph! It's lak as how you gwine ter lose yourn," grumbled Uncle Zeke.

Kate mounted and, holding out her hand to the old man, said:

"Goodbye; thank you, Uncle Zeke. Please, please don't let anybody know where I have gone. You know how anxious Papa is always and he would be so worried."

"Yo' Ung Zeke ain' neber gwine tell; no, not ef his ole tongue gits paddleized stiff en stark. But he's comin' 'long wid you, Honey, en ef he cyan't keep up wid you he kin come 'long behimst you en pick you up ef you draps off. He don' hab ter stay home ter keep no secrets."

Lightning took the low fence at a bound, Uncle Zeke mounting Old Grey and following with great effort though with less rapidity.

There was a fork in the road and when Kate came to it she paused a moment. Both led to Brightview, the left circuitous and requiring more time, the right shorter and beset by obstacles. She turned to the right and had ridden a short distance when she heard voices and the tramp of horses behind her. The tramping ceased and she heard the riders discussing the question of which path to take. After a short parley they rode to the left.

"I'd jes' lak ter know which road dat chile done tuk," said Uncle Zeke riding up to the fork. "One er de roads is de longes' en she wuz natchelly in a hurry, but den she knowed de shortes' one wuz dang'ous en 'pear lak she wouldn' a tuk dat one no matter how big a scurry she wuz in, en 'sides de snyars en pitfalls dar's a sedgebresh fence ter jump en a branch ter fo'de. No, she mus' er tuk de yudder one, en ef she did she's miles en miles away by now, but I knows how ter come up wid her. Dar ain' nuttin' 'bout dis yer nak er woods yo' Ung Zeke don' know fum ale ter izzard. Get up dar, Ole Grey! Pick up yo' foots en get ret 'long ter de cross-road en we'll come 'pon a paf dat meks a nigh cut ter dis lef' hand road 'fo' she gits dar."

Old Grey obeyed and soon reached the cross-roads.

"Huh! Listen! Dat ain' li'le Missus. She don' neber talk ter de Debil en needer do she talk lak dat ter a dumb creeter en needer would a dumb creeter be talkin' back ter her. Den ag'in, she ain' got no sich survigous voice soundin' lak Br'er B'ar wid a bad cold. No, dey's mens a talkin' en Yankee mens at dat, fer I yeared one er 'em say dey guess' dat's de ret road. Well, *I'll* he'p 'em find de way. I 'members when de onsartin man went down fum Jewslum ter Jerrycho en fell 'mongst de thorns en dey sprung up en scratched him en a good Saracem come 'long en showed 'im de way. Ole Zeke gwine be a good Saracem now en gwine show dese Yanks de way ter Jerrycho, too."

Impelled by this philanthropic purpose Uncle Zeke rode forward to the leader of the party.

"Sarvent, Marser. 'Pear lak you-alls is strangers in dese parts. Is dar anyt'ing de ole man kin do fer you?"

"You can tell us the way to Brightview if you will."

"I sho'ly kin do dat, Marser, fer I knows ebby blade er grass in dese parts, speshly Brightview, en de shortes' way, Marser."

"Yes, the shortest way; be quick."

"Yas, sah, Marser, but de shortes' way sometimes is de longes'. Well, you see dat paf dat runs 'long 'roun' by de poplar tree wid de big white streak runnin' up en down whar de lightnin' struck en killed daid dat same night dat ole Missus died wid ammonia in her breas' jamby twenty years ago come naix' fodder-pullin' time, en de ole Marser he —"

"Never mind about your old Master."

"Well, suh, de paf goes 'way 'roun' on turrer side er de tree 'long pas' a hill whar dar's a ha'nted house standin' whar ole Marse Jerry Jones libed en whar he kilt a man en dey say dat de ha'nt comes back uver night en —"

"Oh, shoot the ha'nt!"

"Yas, suh; lots er folks is tried ter shoot it but 'pear lak dey cyan't neber hit it. De bullets dey jes' flies ret th'oo de ha'nt's close en comes out on turrer side er him en de ha'nt he jes' goes ret on lak nuttin' had happened."

"Well, cut it, then, and come to the point and tell us about the road."

"Well, suh, den you goes on twel you comes ter a riber en den you fodes th'oo de riber kaze dar ain' no bridge dar."

"How soon will that bring us to Brightview?"

"Well, I should say ef you goes dat 'way 'twould bring you dar in 'bout a hun'ed yeahs; dat is, ef 'twan't fer de water. Considerin' de water I don' know how long 'twould tek. You mought hab ter go 'roun' de yeth en come up turrer way."

"Confound you! What do you mean by telling us all this rigmarole?"

"I wuz tellin' you dat way, Marser, kaze I wuz skeered you mought go dat way en git los'. Dat's de way fer you *not* ter go."

"Perhaps you could tell us the way we can go, and for heaven's sake, don't take us around by Jupiter if you can help it, for we are in a hurry."

"Yas, suh, I's in a hurry, too, en I don' know whar dat gemman, Marse Jup'ter, libs. He ain' no 'quaintance er we-alls, so I couldn' ca'y you 'long by his house ef I tried. Anyhow, ef you'll tek de road ter de ret en keep on twel you come ter a road dat branches off fum dat road ter de lef' en ter de ret en you tek de lef' hand road you'll git dar, sho'."

"I wonder if you are telling us the truth, old man."

"You kin b'liebe me er not, Marser, jes' ez you choosen, but my w'ite folks brung me up ter t'ink dat a lie is a abomination ter de Lawd (en a ve'y present he'p in time er trouble), en I natchelly 'spises a sto'y-teller."

"You look trustworthy, so I won't doubt you. Here's a shinplaster for you. I suppose, though, you would rather have Confederate money."

"No, suh; money's money ter ole Zeke en he suttinly is much 'bleeged ter you. Ef you eber wan's de ole man you knows whar ter fin' 'im. Far'well ter you, Marser. I's gwine th'oo de woods turrer way."

Uncle Zeke watched the soldiers file off in the direction he had pointed out to them.

"Huh! Lak ter see 'em git ter Brightview dat way. De Lawd knows whar dey'll come out at. Li'le Missus t'ink ole Zeke ain' no use on dis yer ride! Tell you whut, de snail he don' trabel much on a prize race, but somehow he's moughty sho' ter git dar, en de lark a fleein' en a floppin' on de wings er de mornin's lakly ter git shoot by de hunter, en de ole hyar mought bruk his laig er git cotch by de houn's. But de sly ole tar'pin en snail, — don' nobody spec' dem en dey gits dar."

Uncle Zeke ambled on his way, satisfied that one young Confederate officer owed his life to him.

CHAPTER VIII

THE LIGHTS OF BRIGHTVIEW

KATE was riding along the forest path when a dark form emerged from a clump of trees and two long arms were brandished aloft. Lightning swerved aside and his quick movement nearly unseated his rider.

"Don't be afraid, child. It is only your friend, the old Hermit, who comes to serve you. Your mission is needless, Pearl of the Mist. You are riding through the forest at this strange hour to save Jasper Carrington from the Yankees. His danger lies not there, but here, nearer home. He has an enemy *because of you.* Tell him to ride with all speed and to watch the shadows that follow him through the woods to-night."

"Thank you, and God bless you. I will give him your message."

She smiled at the faith which lingered with her from the days of her childhood when the old Hermit had been half terror and half guide for her, and the smile had not vanished when, glancing back, she saw the faintly defined form of a horseman following her. Leaning forward she whispered to Lightning and, dashing across the glade, entered the driveway of Brightview.

"Is that you, Uncle Jerry?" she asked, as an old man sleepily answered her summons.

"Who dat Ung Jerryin' me dis time o' night?"

"It's your Miss Kate, Uncle Jerry. Don't you know me?"

"Yas'm; 'co'se I knows you now; dat is, ef I knows it's you, but de night time en de sleepy-haidedness meks my knowin' mighty unsartin. So dat's hoccome I ax you who is you? En now I ax you how is you?"

"I am very well, thank you, Uncle Jerry, and I hope that you are well."

"No'm; de ole man ain' so well; he's got a mighty misery in de back. But ainchu skeered, Miss Kate, some er dese Yankees gwine 'scrip' dis yer li'le filly er yone? You know, dey's done 'scrip' ebby hoss dat's any 'count in de whole neighborhood."

"No, Uncle Jerry; I have a permit from Colonel Dodge to keep him."

The low-branching trees bordering the path touched Kate and dripped moon-kissed drops of rain upon her as she passed. Jasper Carrington opened the door to her light knock, exclaiming in surprise:

"Why, Miss Kate! How on earth did you get here, at this hour, too?"

Then a pretty girl ran out and kissed her and a sweet-faced matron came forward and took her into her arms, saying:

"We were just speaking of you, dear Kate."

"Her hands are cold. Mother, please give her some of this old Madeira that you have hidden away through all these years, and just brought up tonight in honor of your scapegrace son."

Kate drank the wine, declaring that she was neither cold nor tired and did not need anything, though her pale cheeks belied her words.

"You know I was going to see you tomorrow."

"Yes, I knew you were, and I came here to tell you not to come, for there is a detachment of Yankees after you. Uncle Zeke heard them planning it; and you must not stay here, either, a minute longer than you can help. They said you waylaid their messenger and took the dispatches, and that they regarded you as a dangerous character. You see, dear, your suddenness surprises them and they would be more comfortable if you went North for a time."

"There is something else, too," said Kate, as Jasper, having yielded to the wishes of all, was going. "Be cautious as you ride through the woods to-night, and be careful wherever you are, for there is a shadow on your pathway that threatens a greater evil to you than the Yankees."

"How do you know this, my little prophet?"

"The Hermit told me, and then — then — I saw the shadow myself following along my pathway; so, please, please, be careful."

"I am not afraid, but for your sake, dearest, I will try."

He looked back at her as he rode away into the starry silence of the night, and said laughingly:

"I declare, I am falling into a belief in hermits and shadows, and had *she* warned me that a sheeted specter was on my track I should have looked for it with perfect confidence."

The witchery of the night-shrouded forest

enwrapped him and he fell a-dreaming. The woodsy odors clung around him with myriad hands of enchantment. A bird awakened and trilled out a greeting to the night. He passed a narrow path that made a detour into the woods and came back to the main road a short distance ahead. A man who was following him came to this point and plunged into the side path. At the cross-road he awaited the approach of Carrington, who was awakened from his reverie by the whiz of a ball over his head.

"When you have succeeded in emptying your pistol at me you will please be so good as to explain who you are and why you are making so unskilful an effort to murder a man in the dark. Take all the time you want and don't be frightened. I have no pistol, and would not stain my sword with the blood of a coward."

The dark horseman had come near and the misty light drifting across the pathway fell on his face.

"Do you suppose that if I had taken serious aim I could not have put a bullet through your head as easily as over your hat? I merely wished to arrest your attention."

"Oh, I see you now. No need to tell me who you are. Every man in the South knows Campo, who saved his life by betraying his countrymen. I dare say you can shoot. It is a ruffianly sport enough. The worst I have ever heard about your shooting is that it is in the wrong direction."

Campo threw his pistol to the ground.

"I have a sword. You have called me coward and traitor. That means that one of us must die. You cannot refuse me the satisfaction of learning which one it is to be."

"The truth does not demand satisfaction; it is its own justification."

"At least, you must defend yourself," cried Campo drawing his sword and riding fiercely upon Jasper.

Campo was reckless and made wild lunges that fell wide of their mark. Jasper struck the sword from his grasp and the horse, frightened, promptly threw Campo and dashed off across the moonlit sward.

The dawn was staining the east with a pink light shot with golden arrows when Carrington rode by the pickets guarding the camp. He dismounted in front of his tent as the drums sounded the reveille:

I can't get 'em up, I can't get 'em up,
I can't get 'em up in the morning;
I can't get 'em up, I can't get 'em up,
I can't get 'em up at all.

From his own tent came a repetition of the call, clear, full, repeated in bugle tones and ending in a prolonged note which appealed to him with a force he had never understood. Then the curtain of the tent was lifted and Old Pete greeted him with a cry of joy.

"I knowed dat wuz you, Marse Jasper. Ole Pete's call meks 'im see t'ings 'fo' he sees 'em. En I took up my bugle en bugled fer you. Ya-a-s, Marse Jasper, ef I knowed you wuz daid er wounded, air' one, ole Pete would bugle fer you en listen fer de answer, den bugle ag'in en listen, kaze ef de bref is lef' yo' body en dumbed yo' tongue yo' sperit wouldn' git dumbed; *dat* would answer ole Pete."

"I think I should know your bugle call, Pete, too, dead or alive. But here is something from my mother; here is a package also from some one else. 'Give it to Uncle Pete,' she said, 'and tell him not to forget my message.'"

"'Tain't no use callin' no names, Marse Jasper, en ole Pete ain' neber gwine ter fergit de message dat she g'in 'im ter put in bugle langwidge fer her, — en dat las' bugle soun' wuz de message, Marse Jasper."

Throwing his bridle to Pete he entered the central tent. Darkness yet lingered inside and on a small table was a tallow candle which had burned nearly down to the wooden block that served as a candlestick. Its wavering light glimmered over a map spread upon the table, above which two men were bending in puzzled study, a Major-General seated on a camp-chair and a Brigadier looking over his shoulder.

The Brigadier was tall and rugged, with dark face deeply marked, as if each experience of life had engraved its line in the history written on his countenance. There was nothing of the reckless dash of the enthusiastic warrior in his aspect, yet one looking at him felt that when the time should come he would lead a forlorn hope to the mouth of the guns and fall before them. It must have been in a spasmodic ebullition of youthful spirits that he had made an onslaught upon his comrade, Jubal A. Early, at West Point and had been expelled from that venerable institution for such premature display of valor.

The man sitting at the table leaned back and looked up at his companion.

"Do you know, Armistead," he said, "I am learning the true value of a war map."

"Delighted to know that it *has* a value, Pickett. I have always thought that the one exception to the theory set forth by the poet, 'Nothing walks with aimless feet,' was the man who attempted to follow a war map."

"Just so. The real value of a war map is in pointing out with definiteness one of the many imaginable conformations of the country and setting it beyond the limits of the possible, leaving us free range to choose among the rest. I used to fancy that if an Earth-Man should be turned loose on Jupiter instinct would lead him somewhere. Since this war began I have learned more about the limitations of the race. Once on the Chickahominy I sent for immediate re-enforcements. A detachment of picked men started out under the leadership of one of the most accomplished officers in the service. They marched all night and in the morning found themselves in sight of the camp from which they had started."

"What had become of you, Pickett, in the meantime?"

"I had caught another detachment, which had been ordered northward and had traveled due south till it accidentally fell in with me. Yet our men have hunted over this region since the days of their infancy. Ah, here is Colonel Carrington."

Jasper saluted and handed a paper to the General.

"Thank you, Colonel. You carried my message promptly and have returned earlier than I expected."

"My return was hastened, General, by the necessity of declining a pressing invitation from our Northern friends to remain with them for a time."

"Northern hospitality is occasionally embarrassing to the busy Southerner in haste to get on with his work. I commend your strength of mind in resisting their fascinations, Colonel."

Jasper saluted and withdrew, returning to his tent, where Pete had prepared a breakfast that did honor to his title of Commissary-General.

CHAPTER IX

ON WITH THE DANCE

WHEN Kate returned home the next morning she found her father in his office, leaning back in his big armchair smoking a fig-stemmed corn-cob pipe. A young man whose face she could not see was talking to him. Black Pomp was sitting on the floor making other pipes of corn-cobs and fitting them to long, fragrant fig-stems.

"Hallo, hallo! here comes my Katydid. Where have you been, you little runaway? Nobody on the plantation could tell me where you were. Come, Lady-bird; account for your early morning ride. But first, here is a surprise for you."

"How do you do, Cousin Kate?" said the "surprise." "I am so glad to see you. But you did not expect me, did you?"

"Garnett! How lovely, lovely to see you again! How and when did you come?"

"We are not so very far away and I asked permission to run over. I was so hungry for a sight of home folks."

"How does it go, Garnett, dear? Is it very terrible?"

"Yes. God only knows how terrible. But I could not bear not to be among the others. There has never been a war in our country without a Phillips in it fighting for his flag."

"The fight was never for a flag, but for an idea," said Colonel Marshall. "The old idea still lives, sheltered under our new flag. A sectional party elected a sectional President, who declared war without the authority of Congress and invaded the sovereign States, whose only offense was that they asserted their right and power to fight for their own Union under the Constitution which their forefathers had made."

"If you and my cousin will excuse me I'll go and change my habit while you discuss flags, but remember there is but one flag for me, the Stars and Bars, and but one idea, freedom."

Catherine waved her hand to them and passed out into the hall and up the stairway, the gaze of the young man following her till she disappeared.

"God bless the women!" chuckled the old Colonel. "They will save the South in spite of the devil. If you only had a sweetheart now, Garnett,—a true and patriotic Southern girl like your cousin."

Garnett looked over the head of Pomp and across a sun-bathed slope hedged by a dark belt of woods. He did not see the trees nor the slope nor the sun. He saw only a radiant face with a dazzle of deep eyes, — the same eyes that had smiled back at him as Catherine went up the stairway.

"Here is a rosebud for each of you," said Kate, returning with a Jacqueminot pinned at the throat of her white dress and two buds in her hand. "Guess what is in store for you, Cousin; I am going to take you to Nannie Wickham's ball to-night."

"Could you get an invitation for me at this late hour?"

"Invitation? They would tear my hair out if I did not bring you. How delightful to dance with the dear soldiers who come in their uniforms and look, — oh, so handsome! Just as you do," curtseying elaborately. "The uniforms may be somewhat dingy from hard wear, to be sure, but nothing can keep a Confederate soldier from being beautiful, and — well, there never were such dancers anywhere else in the whole world."

"I didn't know any but our crowd were within a day's march."

"Yes; one of the regiments is camped down in the glen for the night on the way to join Pickett's Division. The ball is given for them. All we are afraid of is that the Yankees will find it out, but I don't think they will. They've sent too many men north to take any risks. Usually we have dry bread balls, but Ung Lige found a bee-tree today and brought home a great pan of honey and we are to have a honey-pulling to-night."

"How delightful! And you are to wear a white dress and a red rose?"

"Of course; they are my colors."

"They are my colors, too."

That evening he was at the foot of the stairs when Kate came down looking like a white cloud floating against a dun-gray curtain of space. At the belt of her soft white dress was massed a cluster of Giant of Battle roses.

"What wondrous draperies you war-time maidens wear."

"This robe belonged to one of my grandmothers away back in the centuries. She wore it at a ball in the court of Louis the Superb and danced with Prince Condé. But the roses bloomed today and belong to the sunshine."

"The roses blossomed in the sunshine of your presence and belong to you. As for the robe, I venture the Court Lady did not look half so pretty in it as her descendant does."

"Condé could tell you better than that, flatterer, but just you wait till you see Nannie Wickham. She has a really and truly new dress, smuggled through the lines. It is a dream and so is she, and you shall fall in love with her."

"That is impossible; I have fallen in love."

"Oh, but old love affairs do not count."

The carriage rolled through the Southern dusk along a dreamful lane, and Kate chatted gaily with the recklessness of youth that dances lightly on whether cannons boom or doves of peace coo softly. Soon they were at Nannie's gate and in a moment were whirled away in the light and glow and laughter and music.

"It seems to me that we are dancing on the rim of a volcano," said Garnett as he walked with Nannie Wickham between dances.

"Yes; some people have been calling us frivolous and saying growly things about our dancing lately, because of the increasing anxiety since General Pemberton has been repulsed at Jackson and Vicksburg is in danger. But General Joe Johnston is there and everything must come out right where he is. My old mammy shakes her head when she dresses me and says she's 'had signs an' we-all better be havin' pra'r-meetin's, steader dancin'.'"

Nannie stopped suddenly.

"What was that? Listen! Didn't you hear something?"

"Yes; it sounded like the tramp of horses and the clank of steel."

Hurrying back to the ball-room they ran upon Pomp, whose eyes revolved in an ecstasy of terror as he warningly cried out:

"Hi-sh. You-all —sh —sh — sh — I tole you so. Dey's comin' — dey's comin' — yas dey's jamby 'pon top er we-alls dis minute, wi'le we-all's dancin' en frolickin' — I done tole you so! I tole you so!"

"Told us what? Who's coming?" sternly asked Colonel Wilmer. "Stop your stammering and speak out!"

"De Yanks, Marse Kunnel. Dey's outside

dis minute. You-all better run er hide er do sumpn 'fo' you gits hurt."

"Lieutenant Hetherington, signal to camp for the boys at once. Ladies to the upper rooms! Lights out!"

Awed by the Colonel's commanding tone, the girls fled upstairs. Pomp crawled under the table. Over the dancing hall darkness fell and "Fiddling Cæsar" stood with uplifted bow as if petrified in "Swing your pardners, hands all round!"

"Look! There is a flag of truce," said Nannie. "They are coming to summon us to surrender."

"We will die first!" asserted Catherine valiantly.

"That's easy enough to talk about," replied Nannie dolorously.

"Colonel Dasham calls upon the Confederate officers within to surrender and thereby save the house from destruction!" called out the bearer of the flag of truce.

"My compliments to Colonel Dasham and tell him that we are much obliged but that we can protect the house without his assistance."

The truce withdrew and soon a hailstorm of shot was heard. Answering shots were fired from the windows and one of the assailants fell and was carried away.

"Poor fellow!" said Kate, always ready to sympathize with misfortune. "I hope he is not hurt much. We have the advantage, you see. We are in the dark and they in full moonlight."

"Oh, me! they are separating and some are going to the back door," whispered Nannie, "and, listen; the rest of the boys are coming."

The men from camp came swinging around the curve and the girls waved their handkerchiefs from the window.

A shower of rifle-balls greeted the attacking party and the detachment at the rear door joined their comrades in front. After a skirmish they retreated to the woods, pursued by the Lieutenant and his men from the camp and followed by the cheers of the Colonel's forces, in which the girls joined heartily.

"Hurrah, girls!" cried Kate. "We have won a battle."

"Were you frightened?" asked Colonel Wilmer, coming up the stairway, followed by Garnett.

"Frightened?" replied Kate. "It was glorious! But that poor fellow who was shot — where is he?"

"I don't think there was much blood shed, — at any rate, no wounded left on the field."

Upon their return to Magnolia Lawn Kate and Garnett stopped for a moment upon the veranda and looked out into the moonlight where the pines were black against the silvery wall.

"Why do beautiful things seem sad?" asked Kate as a south wind swept up from the river and, lifting a branch of the rose-vine, brushed it across her cheek.

"I suppose it is because we cannot take all their beauty into eyes and heart at once. There is a reason, though, why all this" — stretching his arms out toward river and wide white space — "is especially sad to me to-night, because I must say goodbye — perhaps for an even longer separation than before."

"Oh, I hope not, — surely not."

"I go to-night to join Armistead's Brigade."

"Oh, I am so sorry! No, I don't mean that I am sorry, either — I'm glad. It is just what I would have you do. And then — you will see — Jasper."

"Jasper — Jasper?"

She looked up shyly.

"Yes; didn't you know?"

He was silent for an instant, gazing out into the blackness of the pines. Then he said gently:

"I — I congratulate you, Cousin mine."

"I knew you would. Now I want you to do something for me."

"Anything, to the extent of my power, Kate."

"Jasper is so brave, so daring, so almost reckless, — I want you to make friends with him and guard him from the dangers that he will not see — take care of him for me."

Her uplifted face glowed with love and entreaty, but in his eyes was the light of self-abnegation. He took her hand and lifted it to his lips.

"If my life can purchase his it will be freely given, for your sake."

"Thank you. Both lives will come back to make me happy."

"*If God wills,*" he said solemnly.

She watched him ride down the lane, looking after him until he was hidden in the forest, the winding empty road lying black across the moonlight.

CHAPTER X

FROM THE FRONT

KATE was reading a letter to her father.

HEADQUARTERS ARMY OF NORTHERN VIRGINIA
June 9, 1863.

"DEAREST COUSIN MINE:

On the 3d of June we joined Longstreet on his way to Culpeper Courthouse. Remembering my promise to you, the first thing I did after necessary preliminaries was to hunt up Colonel Carrington and give him your letter and message. Allow me to congratulate you on your good judgment. The Colonel is a fine fellow.

"Longstreet, the Apostle, 'Old Peter,' as the soldiers have nicknamed him, seems to have all the attributes of a great soldier,—not the dash perhaps of him who fell at Chancellorsville, but he has care, caution, and bull-doggedness, which are equally necessary, and all the country knows how brave he is.

"But the soldier who thrills me as no other can is the Commander of our Division, General Pickett. It is an inspiration to see him ride along our lines, his wavy, dark hair floating out on the wind, the boys cheering as if they would never stop. He answers with a salute, lifts his cap and, holding it above his head, rides on in his courtly way, sitting his horse as I used to fancy King Arthur did, in the days when we read of him together, you and I, in our poetry books.

"I had pictured him to myself as very tall, but he is of medium height and looks tall because he is perfectly formed and carries himself erectly. I supposed that he had a great voice which sounded as if it might come from the depths of the earth, but his tones are soft and musical. He looks young to have been before the cannon's mouth for seventeen years. People who know him well say that he is equally at home in storming a height and in playing the guitar and singing a serenade to his ladylove. One of his staff officers said that when a friend of our General was going North and asked what he should bring for him, he replied, 'A bottle of heliotrope and a bottle of new-mown hay.' To a rugged chap like me that might sound a little dandyish if I did not know that the next day at the head of his men, with his right arm hanging helpless and his left waving his sword, he dashed up a hill blazing with cannon and won the fight.

"General Scott said: — 'Generals nowadays can be made out of anything, but good men are hard to get.' Are not we fortunate in having so good a man in a General?

"Yesterday General Lee reviewed Stuart's cavalry. They say it was a brilliant sight. The Red Fox, as they call Stuart, because he is a rosy blonde and because he has a light and foxy way of scampering across country, has the best riders in the world and people say that he is the finest cavalry leader anywhere. He is the most unexpected man in the Confederacy. He appears and disappears as if moved by electric wires. The enemy lays the deepest traps for him and finds when the time comes to spring them that he has vanished. Then he suddenly darts out in another place so far away that it would seem that his horse must wear seven-league shoes. He doubles and curves in such a wonderful way that nobody can ever imagine where he will be next. As a means of developing alert mental action in his soldiery the General of the Army of the Potomac has taken to offering prizes for the best conjecture as to where Stuart will appear. So, at least, I was told by a jovial Yankee who kept company with us until he eloped with the Captain's horse one night in a moment of inadvertence on the part of the gentleman who had been appointed to see that he had a good time.

"We have come to the end of a long day's march and have gone into camp to spend a rainy night. A Lieutenant who pursues war as a pastime and music as a business is singing 'Oh, Susannah, don't you cry for me,' and accompanying himself on the banjo. Two others are exchanging reminiscences of Chancellorsville and incidentally breaking forth uproariously into Stuart's lyric, 'Old Joe Hooker, come out of the wilderness.' A game of cards is progressing in a lively manner and my train of thought is now and then thrown off the track by shrieks of joy from one side and howls of despair from the other. Two enthusiastic military students are laying out a plan of battle and every few moments falling into what promises to be mortal combat over a disputed fortification. The beauty of my chirography is due to the fact that I am seated on a camp-chair, holding my paper on my knee and writing with a pen the point of which has acquired an upward curve from hard usage, the whole scene being illuminated by a tallow candle in frequent need of being snuffed.

"I am not likely soon again to strike such favorable circumstances for collecting and transcribing my thoughts, but you must not allow that fact to curtail my supply of letters from home. You don't know how hungry a fellow is for the sound of a sweet home voice and the sight of a dear home face and the touch of a tender home hand.

"I have had a letter from my mother,—poor dear little mother. Torn by divided affections and anxious about so many sorrowful and perilous things, I think of her with sadness that grows heavier each day. I wish that you could go to her or that she might come to you, but I suppose that is hardly possible. So all you can do is to seize upon every opportunity of writing a sweet and comforting letter to her and one sometimes, too, to your

"Cousin Garnett."

As Kate finished the letter, she looked up wistfully at her father and said:

"Oh, father, if I had only been a boy!"

"Thank the Lord that you are not a boy, my daughter."

"Do you love me better as I am, Papa, dear?"

"If you were my son instead of my daughter, even loved as you are now, I should give you up though it were to death."

CHAPTER XI

WAITING

THE Army of Northern Virginia was on the road to Chambersburg. The march was necessarily slow, for not even the Commander-in-Chief had any information regarding the Federal movements.

Colonel Carrington had sent for Garnett and they were side by side.

"There is something I intended to tell you," Garnett said, "about that Campo fellow, who manages to keep himself tangled up with us in the most incomprehensible way. I did not tell you of the first time. It was when I had been mistaken for you and put into a prison-house to wait for him to pass upon my identity. The next time was that day in the skirmish as we crossed the line; he tried to stick a sword into you. I thank God I was a shade too quick for him and he disappeared just as you downed that Yankee Captain."

"He is the meanest kind of a scoundrel and coward," said Jasper. "Thanks to your friendly offices, he gives you more trouble than he does me, for which I am sorry. But I am very grateful to you for staying his murderous hand."

They passed by fields in which the ripening grain promised a veritable harvest of gold. Garnett thought of the desolate waste through which he had marched in Virginia. The fields were there, ready to yield their treasures to the skilful touch. But the tillers were gone and there was no hand stretched out to help those barren acres to blossom forth and fulfil their hospitable mission.

The orchards, in which the burdened branches almost touched the ground with the weight of their fruitage, reminded Garnett of an orchard where in boyhood he gathered apples, red and golden. On the road to Maryland he had seen it again. It was an old battlefield now and the fire-scarred trees stretched their ghostly gray arms to the sky as if asking the vengeance of heaven on the wickedness of man.

In this fair and prosperous land homelike dwellings nestled away in the greenery of beautiful trees and looked bewitchingly out from their leafy bowers. In Virginia the Army had passed by piles of ashes where in the olden days stately homes had given Garnett loving welcome, by lonely deserted houses that had once been sunny and bright. As they were passing one of these mansions an old negro hobbled out to greet Garnett.

"Wait, Marse Garnett, drap out ef you kin. I've been waitin' fer you. I knowed some er de ole time folks what used ter visit we-all 'ud be comin' th'oo somewhar wid de army en I's been watchin' en watchin' wheneber dey'd be a marchin' by. I's de onlyes' one lef' on de ole place now en I ain' got nuttin' 'tall ter fetch you sepn some roas' 'taters en a piece er ole hyar I cotch in de woods yistidy en cooked."

The tears sprang to Garnett's eyes. Only an old servant with his love-gift left to greet him.

Now along the road bordered with plenty they came to Chambersburg, where there was none to give them welcome or even a passing word. They marched quietly through the town, their band silent, for the order was that no music should be played lest it might offend the citizens. Through an almost deserted street between rows of closed houses they went till they were near the limits of the town. Here several girls who had been drawn by curiosity to the veranda of a cottage asked for some music and were greeted with "The girl I left behind me," "Home, sweet Home," and "Auld lang syne." But these non-committal strains were not their idea of Southern music, and they called for "Dixie." They were answered by the gentle notes of "Her bright smile haunts me still," and the Division marched on to camp.

The men carried away pleasant memories of the little town among the hills, for the dwellers therein did not long resist the courtesy and kindness of the Confederate leader and when marching orders came many a word of good-will followed the Southern soldiers to Gettysburg.

Hands of the dead, far-away hands of the living, dream hands that dwelt but in imagination, all seemed stretched forth to Garnett and Jasper as the old Division marched through the woods in which they had halted to await the morning summons to the field. Faces looked out at them from behind the trees, — faces shrined in their hearts by memory, faces hovering mistily on the far horizon of their fancy. Was there ever so ghostly a wood as this that lay between their night's bivouac and the fighting line at Gettysburg? Only the rustling of feet upon the grass broke the stillness. Yet was the silence full of sound — whispers of voices and the echoes of yesterday's guns thrilling on the air.

When they passed through the line of woods fringing Seminary Ridge, morning yet waited behind the hills. The men lay in the long grass and the trees kept guard around them. The weary soldiers held the attitudes into which they had thrown themselves as if they might have been stone figures cast aside by an impatient sculptor. Some fell asleep. Others waited grimly for the dawn, — the strangest dawn that ever gloomed into their lives.

Garnett, resting on his elbow, looked toward the east where a ridge slightly overtopped the ground on which he lay. What was between his fancy could not show. How the day had gone he did not know. No tidings had come from the battle except the dull echoes of the guns that had shivered the air on the road from Chambersburg.

The crash of Gary's pistol broke the stillness and sent echoes reverberating among the hills. Day was ushered in with the ominous greeting which befitted its awful destiny.

Some of the men, aroused from their half slumbers, looked in the direction from which the sound came. A quiver as of a suddenly awakened force ready for combat thrilled through Garnett's veins. The man who had been at Antietam lay quiet. He was still asleep.

A deeper silence fell over the ridge, — a stillness that stretched out in awesome gloom to the sky and reached down to earth.

After what seemed to Garnett a soundless eternity the silence was broken by the tread of horses coming down the line. In the shimmer of dawn he could see the faces of the riders and the color of their horses as they rode along.

Every man in the Army knew the powerful gray that carried the Commander. He and his rider were one, so closely were they identified with all the exploits of the Army of the South. Garnett never saw that stately figure mounted on "Traveler" without a glow of pride.

Beside him was a taller, heavier man, he who bore worthily the title of "Old War Horse," affectionately bestowed upon him by the Commanding General.

Garnett's glance swept over these two figures and centered on the third of the group, wondering, as he had many times, wherein lay the power of that man. Smaller than the two with whom he rode, slight, delicately formed, he was in strong contrast to his companions. He sat his horse with the grace of one who rides to win a guerdon from the hand of beauty rather than to meet the foe in deadly conflict. His face was almost womanly fair and his soft dark hair swept backward in the morning wind like the hair Garnett remembered in a picture at Magnolia Lawn of a minstrel who sang of the past in the ancient halls of his ancestors. Were ever grace and delicacy so opposed to the rude idea of war as in his person and life history? Yet men went down into the infernal pit of battle and were drowned in seas of fire for love of him and the glory of following where he led.

Having been strictly enjoined to silence, the men dared not cheer. They arose and stood reverently with bared heads as the horsemen rode down the line in silent review, — the last death review, — and every eye of the long line was on the slender man who rode the black charger and held his cap lifted above his head. Thus they watched their leader till the shadows hid him from view.

In the grass in front of the forest line they lay through hours of beating sun. There were no sleepers now. Each man was awake to the heat that poured upon him as from a burning cauldron. Occasionally one moved restlessly. Now and then there was a whisper to a comrade.

"The Baby," the youngest soldier in the regiment, crept close to Garnett and held his hand. His yellow curls were matted damply over his head. In his eyes were depths of unspoken sadness.

"I want you to do something for me, for, somehow, I feel that I shall not live out this day."

"Nonsense, boy, nonsense. You will live to be gray-bearded, and some day you will hold your grandchildren on your knee and tell them of how we won a glorious victory and saved our Southland."

The boy shook his head sadly.

"Men in our way of life sometimes know; there is something in their hearts that tells them."

"Brace up, my boy; brace up. We all have a feeling of that kind in the presence of a great danger. We come up out of the conflict with hearts stronger because of the trial and lives better for the victory."

"I don't know what it is, but I feel that my heart will be stilled in this battle, and when you march back to the Capital of our new Nation won't you find my mother and tell her about me and give her this letter? Oh, tell her how dearly I love her and that the proudest thing in her boy's life is in trying to be worthy of her and in giving the life she gave him to his country."

"I'll take the letter, of course, boy, but suppose I should still keep you company at the end of the day?"

There was a long silence and then the man who had been at Antietam turned over and growled:

"By George, fellows, I say, this makes me think of what Tom August said to Squire Minturn."

"What's that?" asked the man next him.

WAITING

"You know the Squire puts on as many airs as if he'd swallowed a hurricane and it was breaking out on him. He met Tom and said in his swell way, 'Well, sir, I suppose your voice is still for war!' And Tom said, 'Yes, Squire, devilish still.'"

CHAPTER XII

"THE BATTLE'S VAN"

The fittest place where man can die
Is where he dies for man.

A CANNON-SHOT shivered the awful silence. While it echoed from the hills another shot thundered out and a cloud of smoke hung over the plain. Then came a crash of artillery and between the two ridges was a blazing sea over which a heavy curtain of smoke waved and tossed tumultuously like a wrack of storm-clouds in a raging wind. The hills trembled with the roar of battle. It was as if warring worlds had rushed together in one stupendous conflict. Through a rolling ocean of smoke and dust flaming arrows darted across the field.

"Them pesky things allus 'pears to be aimin' straight at a feller's eyes," grumbled one of Armistead's men, blinking as a burning shell swept past him.

A man who was lying near leaped suddenly forward and fell, his blood spattering on Garnett's sleeve. The shriek of a shell hurtled by and a little distance from him he saw the earth torn up and heard the dying groans of comrades. Even in the mighty uproar, looking upon the fire and smoke of the most terrific cannonading the world ever knew, Garnett pitied those who had fallen at the threshold of the battle, — who could never go down into that sea of surging flame and wind-tossed smoke and charge the fire-crested heights.

On a hill overlooking the valley was the stately form of the Commander on his powerful gray horse. He turned to Pickett, mounted by his side, and pointed to a clump of trees flanked by a glittering array of artillery and infantry on the ridge opposite.

"General, can you take that height?"

"I can, sir, if it *can* be taken."

While the roar of the cannon filled the valley and fiery fuses were still darting through the blackness, General Pickett came down the line. The men sprang to their feet and saluted as he, pointing to the flame-crowned hill, explained what they were to do. Cheer after cheer followed him.

Jasper's head was uncovered and a light wind blew his hair back as Garnett looked at him leading his regiment, and across the distance heard a sweet voice say:

"Take care of him for me, — take care of him in camp and on field!"

"I promise!" he had said with all the solemnity with which he would have made a vow to his Creator.

His pledge to the woman he loved came back to him with the touch of the south wind and he renewed the promise in his heart to guard with his own life the man who was dear to her. What, after all, was his life in comparison with the happiness of her loving heart?

A stray shell from the opposite ridge struck down a soldier at Garnett's side. "The Baby" moved quietly in and the line was unbroken. The boy looked up and smiled as a child might have looked at his protector. Garnett took his hand and pressed it affectionately. It seemed a mournful prophecy that death should have placed them side by side as they were about to march down the fatal slope.

The soldier in front of him turned to a comrade and said:

"We are to charge that height?"

"Yes."

Fixing his gaze southward he said, "Then this will be a sad day for Virginia," and stretching out his arms he called out solemnly, — " Goodbye, Virginia!" He thought of the little cottage nestling away in the Blue Ridge in that beloved old State which bounded the dreams of his youth and the memories of his manhood.

"Goodbye!" surged through the heart of Garnett, and a radiance of dark eyes and a swaying of a slim young form draped in white, with a crimson Jacqueminot at the throat, was the vision that passed before his eyes as he shut them to the smoke-wreathed valley and the fiery height.

The gaze of Jasper was directed straight forward to the forest of guns on the hill in front. Garnett could see only the set pose of the head with its stern unwavering lines. Maybe that was why all things came to Jasper. Was the same farewell echoing sorrowfully in his heart? Or was he intent only upon scaling that deadly wall beyond?

Garnett watched the graceful form on the black charger as their leader took his place at their head, his long dark hair floating back in the wind.

"Forward!"

Pickett's men started on their death-march. They moved out from the forest calmly and steadily as if drawn up for a grand review. Two great armies watched them in admiring awe. Over on Seminary Hill the man on the gray horse looked on at the costly sacrifice the South was making for its cause. On Cemetery Height the men in blue were silent, watching the majestic scene.

The rhythmic motion of the thousands of tramping feet had so taken possession of Garnett's imagination that he seemed to have been for ages walking in that solemn procession. The resounding tramp, tramp, tramp filled all the world.

Garnett's gaze was fixed on the Commander far away in front, leading his men into the flames of battle with an air of chivalrous lightness and grace such as he might have worn had he led them in picturesque procession to enliven a festal day. He marveled over the daring that could enable a man to maintain a poise like that at the open door of death. He thought of what he had heard a commanding officer say:

"Give George Pickett an order and he will storm the gates of hell."

By the silent batteries the "Old War Horse" stood with General Alexander, of the Artillery, looking with grave face at the long lines moving toward the smoke-shrouded valley. As they filed by he acknowledged with a gesture the salutation of the officers.

At the crest a deadly roar and blinding flash from the guns across the valley met them. All around men were falling, but Garnett kept his eyes fixed upon the gallant figure in front and followed. The vacant places were filled and the line passed on down the slope into open ground through the storm of balls and shells raining from Cemetery Height.

As the smoke lifted, the sad and silent man standing by the batteries saw the solid ranks moving steadily on in symphonic rhythm, their guns flashing in the sun.

"Wright says it is not so hard to go there," said the Artillery Commander. "He was nearly there with his brigade yesterday. The difficulty is to stay there."

General Longstreet looked across at the dark lines of men and guns on the opposite ridge.

"Yes, yes, that is the difficulty," he said.

But the guns? Garnett had looked at them with pride and confidence as he passed. When their bulldog voices sounded across the valley they might serve as the overture to a symphony of triumph.

The guns! That was the anxious thought of the Corps Commander as his gaze followed the men on their descent into the valley of death. He knew why the guns by which he stood were silent as they sullenly looked down upon a movement which they could not support.

"Stop Pickett and replenish the ammunition," he said to the Artillery Commander.

"We can't do that, sir," was the mournful reply. "It would take an hour to distribute it and meanwhile the enemy would improve the time."

Longstreet turned from the silent guns to acknowledge the salute of a tall officer who was leading his brigade down the fatal slope. With a start of surprise he recognized General Garnett, who for days had been following the army in an ambulance. He had made his attendants lift him to the saddle and fasten him there that he might lead his men to the glorious death that blazed before his vision.

General Alexander's heart leaped at the sight of the friend whom he had not seen for months, and following its promptings he went down the line and joined General Garnett and rode side by side with him to the rim of the slope. There he paused and held out his hand.

"Goodbye, and good luck to you, old man," he said.

"A soldier's luck," returned General Garnett with serene uplifted gaze, as if even then he felt the outrushing tide of life-blood which would on that day wash away the fiery letters in which "Kernstown" had been graven upon his valiant heart.

The line reached open ground under a storm of balls from Cemetery Ridge. The gaps the guns had made in the ranks filled up and the solid, living wall went forward as if the dead that covered the ground like the fallen leaves of autumn had added the impulse of their own lives to the strength of their comrades.

A long blue line sprang suddenly up from the grass which had hidden it from view, fired and ran on, loading and turning to shoot again. The battle-flag in front of Garnett fell. Before it reached the ground he took it from the hand of the "Baby," who looked a last farewell and faintly whispered "Remember." Again the ranks closed up and went on unfalteringly.

As Garnett caught the flag one of his comrades sprang forward with the same design. He looked around and saw the smoke-blackened face of the man who had bade farewell to Virginia. Garnett passed the flag to him and they went on together.

"Left oblique!"

Swiftly and steadily they obeyed while a deafening roar filled the valley and a rain of balls swept down from the cannon in front of them. Again were the wide gaps filled as were never such gaps of horror filled in the long story of warfare.

"Front forward!"

Straight down upon the center now — on! — on! — the glory of the battle sweeping around them, enfolding them in a mantle of flame, urging them forward with exultant feet and hearts on fire.

"Forward! Quick march!"

Where the balls fell thickest and the fire seemed to center in a condensed heart of flame Garnett saw the horseman on whom his eyes were fixed pause and look over the field. Like a statue he sat while a leaden hail showered around him. With his comrades Garnett rushed by.

Over the fence that crossed the field they leaped, the line breaking at the moment of clearing, but instantly at command reforming under a fiery storm from the batteries on the heights amid the explosion of shells that filled the air while the cries of the wounded and dying pierced their hearts.

"Faster, men! Faster!" they heard above the roar of the guns and the tramp of the feet. Then the voice fell on silence. General Garnett was dead.

"Come on, boys!" shouted another voice and a sword flashed high in the sun, a hat borne upon its point. The tall, rugged man who carried it aloft pointed to the blazing hill and urged the men forward, his own daring furnishing a magnet that was irresistible.

The leader on the black war-horse stopped on the highroad that crossed the field and sat like a figure of stone, the battle hot around him. A staff officer came back from carrying an order.

"You are losing your spurs, Captain Bright, instead of winning them," said the General.

Captain Bright followed the glance of his leader and saw that his spur had been shot through and was hanging from his boot. The General calmly viewed the scene, his keen eye taking in every movement. The men rushed by and Garnett thrilled with ardor as he saw the motionless, erect figure under the falling shot and bursting shells.

On the other side of the line a man in blue lifted his rifle and took careful aim at the form standing out so boldly against the light. Then he lowered his gun and turned back. Three of his comrades were putting down their guns. "We can't kill a man as brave as that," they said.

Over on the right a gleam of bayonets and a fire of musketry blazed into the faces of the little band. It reeled and fell back, then rallied and pressed on, and the two opposing forces were intermingled, their muskets crossing in fierce combat. Jasper, dismounted, was in front of Garnett, resisting the onslaught of a tall, dark man.

"The Raven!" thought Garnett.

He thrust his sword into the heart of Jasper's assailant, who fell and was trampled under many feet struggling toward the height.

The man who bore the flag fell and Garnett would have stopped to aid him.

"Don't mind me," said the wounded man. "Carry the flag to the front."

A horse came dashing by and the fallen man caught his bridle.

"Like Kendall, I can be a hitching post," he said.

Garnett bore the flag onward.

Over the stone wall and up the hill they followed the sword that flashed a silver path for them till they stood upon the flaming crest. The first line of defenders fell back and Garnett waved his battle-flag over the gun beside which stood the man whose sword-flash had lit the way. In a seething heart of fire he saw the leader fall.

Forced back by the rally of the men on the height, the little remnant of survivors reeled down the hill, Jasper and Garnett together, a storm of bullets following them as they went. Half-way down the slope Jasper fell back and Garnett caught him in his arms. "Jasper, are you hurt, old fellow?"

Jasper made no answer and Garnett carried him on, a mortal faintness seizing him suddenly, but he heeded it not, for above the roar of the guns, the cries of the wounded, the tramp of men and horses he heard a soft voice saying:

"Take care of him for me, — take care of him for me!"

He laid his comrade upon the ground and poured down his throat a drink from his canteen.

"He is not dead. He will not die; cannot, for he has love to live for and it will take him safely back to her."

As he sank upon the ground he heard the sound of hobbling feet and the face of Eagleheart was thrust into his own.

"Eagleheart, old fellow, did you come to tell me goodbye? I know you carried your rider valiantly into the battle till he fell from your back. He could not have gone on without you, for he was too ill to ride any other. Oh, I am proud of you, Eagleheart, and I am glad I lent you to the brave General Garnett. I wonder if he knows that his namesake soldier follows him so soon."

The pathetic brown eyes of Eagleheart looked wistfully into his with insistent appeal. Then Garnett saw that one of his feet was shot off and, led by instinct, he had hobbled to his master.

"Eagleheart, I love you and will do what you ask of me. Goodbye, old fellow."

He drew the pistol from his belt and took sure aim. A long, slow quiver, a deep-drawn sigh, and Eagleheart was at rest.

Garnett moved nearer to Jasper and put his arm over him. He was too weak to lift himself to see how it was with his friend, but he felt that all was right.

A bugle-note floated over the field, faint as if the gentle Muse feared to enter upon the terrible scene, plaintive as if the woes of a universe weighed it down.

"Thank God, that is old Pete; he will find him for her," said Garnett, as he sank into unconsciousness.

"That is old Pete, bugling the dirge in the greatest death-march the world has ever known," thought the leader of the little remnant falling back from the fire-crested height, and as Pete saw the General he involuntarily struck the triumphant note with which he had always greeted him, "See, the conquering hero comes." But memory brought a sorrowful strain into which was woven the tragedy of a glorious and futile effort. Listening, he who had led his men through the storm saw visions as in a cloud, the aspiration of battle, the thrill of the charge. His heart leaped with the impulse of victory, sank with the knowledge of defeat.

Then the bugle tones passed on and soared

above the clank of men surging back from a glorious defeat that held no less of nobility than would have shone in the crown of victory. It caught the heartbreak of wounds and death, the love and longing of passing souls, the agony of *sadder* souls that must remain on earth and *remember*, the woe and horror of that field of destruction, and carried it aloft, mingled with the flower-fragrance of love's farewell and the dawn-glory of the morning heights of eternal life, to beat against the gates of that city where Peace reigns forever.

It came softly to Garnett, as he lay touching the border-land with one hand while the other reached longingly, gropingly, back toward loved ones whom he was leaving. There was a familiar tone in the strain as if it were wafted to him on the winds of long-gone summers. It did not come to him with the terrors of battle, — the darkness of death. He was far away from the world's wars. To him it bore the fragrance of wood-flowers that grew along the paths he had trod in boyhood. It was aglow with the sunlight that bathed a hillside where he used to play. He saw again the long grass waving in the wind. A song came lilting down the years from the parted red lips of a hazel-eyed girl with a forest of song-birds in her throat.

Over toward the sunset the little band had swept down the hill beyond his sight and hearing.

"I have kept my faith, Catherine. I send him back to you and to love," sighed Garnett, as old Pete's notes, bugling for his master, brought him back to consciousness.

He lay still for a time, his lashes sweeping down upon his cheek, and then as his soul took its flight her voice came to him on the golden thread of an old song. A smile lit up his face, he opened his eyes and whispered:

"I knew you would come, sweetheart. I feel the touch of your hand and your sweet eyes are lighting the way for me. Goodbye, — goodb–y–e, K–a–t–e."

CHAPTER XIII

A SHIELD OF FAITH

LIKE a bit of wreckage tossed up from a stormy sea, Jasper lay by the roadside. Through the darkness that environed him he heard a last fond goodbye spoken by a loved voice but he could make no answer. The sound of a bugle called him and he tried to struggle back to light but sank again into shadows.

Old Pete, anxious ever for the fate of the young master whom destiny had confided to him, found him after much bugling and praying and a perilous search.

"Praise de Lawd! Ez soon ez I buckled on de shield er faith I knowed I'd find you, daid er alibe, Marse Jasper, en 'fo' Gord you ain' needer de one ner needer de yudder, en ef yer ain' you en Marse Garnett layin' yer tergedder side by side wid one anudder. I mought a knowed I'd foun' you dat away, dough, fer dar neber wuz no great distance 'twix' you bofe. Lubly in life, in def you ain' 'wided. Scuse me, Marse Jasper, I gwine feel yer heart. T'ank Gawd! T'ank Gawd! It's a beatin' en good en strong. Yo' life is spyared—spyared!"

He turned to Garnett, whose arm was over Jasper's shoulder.

"Praise be ter de Lamb, you ain' daid, needer, Marse Garnett. S'pec' you's jes' got peppered up a li'le, too, wid dem bullets. Well, I ain' neber seed no Marser er mine so bad off dat I couldn' fotch 'im to wid a li'le managin'. I habs ter ax you to scuse me, too, Marse Garnett, but I 'bleeged ter tek yo' arm offn Marse Jasper, so he kin breave better, en you kin, too. Name er gracious! What's dis? Lawd! Lawd! What's de matter wid my ole eyes? Marse Garnett! Marse Garnett! Marse Garnett! Is you daid, Marse Garnett?—daid en smilin' at me lak dat? Well, I neber would a thunk you could be daid en smile lak dat, Marse Garnett. You neber done dat away befo'; neber sence I knowed you; en 'tain' lak you, Marse Garnett, ter go and leabe Marse Jasper by hisse'f. Fergib me, please, suh, fergib yo' ole Pete fer what he's gwine ter do, but he's 'bleeged ter part you en Marse Jasper now sho' 'nough, en hit suttinly do hu't him th'oo en th'oo f'um his gizzard ter his lights ter do it, but ef Marse Jasper comes to en sees you lak dis, den ole Pete gwine hab double trouble ter kyar back ter de home folks. Yas, dar'll be a pyar er daid ones ter moan ober."

So saying, Pete, after listening again at Garnett's heart, lifted him tenderly and carried him away, laying him down gently and taking a mournful leave of him.

"You sho'ly wuz a gemman, Marse Garnett, — a gemman ter de backbone ef eber dar wuz one. You allers had a ninepence raidy in peace time en a shinplaster or a nice crackly Confederick note in war time fer de ole man. Well, you're safe now, Marse Garnett, safe in de bosom er good ole Marse Aberham, whar bullets en bayonets cyan' tetch you no mo' en whar mebbe you mought git sumpn decent fer ter eat. I gwine gib Miss Kate a message fer you. Ole Pete know heap mo' dan you t'ink he know. You cyan' fool ole Pete. He knows dat smile on yo' face wuz fer Miss Kate. Ole Pete's heart is mos' bruk ter leabe you lak dis, Marse Garnett, fer you is mos' lak his own young Marser, but he 'bleeged ter do it fer

Marse Jasper mought come to any minute en I cyan' do you no good now. Goodbye, Marse Garnett, goodbye."

With tears rolling down his cheeks the faithful servant returned to Jasper.

"I knows I kin fetch Marse Jasper back fum de grabe ef I bugles fer him. I gwine try de reveille now: dat's de chune dat weks him mawnin's. Yas, dat's allus weked him fum de soundes' sleep dat a soger knows; dat sleep dat he has w'en he's marched all day en half de night befo'."

No answering look of consciousness came to the still face in response to the stirring notes that had so often aroused the young soldier to the duties of the day.

"What! Dat don' wek you? Well, I gwine buckle on my faith en try sumpn dat will; dat chune Miss Kate totch me ter bugle; dat 'ud fotch you back ef you wuz daid en buried. No, suh, Marse Jasper, you won' lay still w'en dem notes is a floatin' 'roun' you. Ah, hong! — What I say? Gawd bress Miss Kate fer teachin' me dat song! — Gawd be praised dat I hilt on ter de faith!"

Whether the magic of his sweetheart's bugle-song had the power ascribed to it or not, the young Colonel opened his eyes before it was finished.

"Is it time to get up, Pete?"

"Nor, suh; 'tain' time yit, Marse Jasper. Den ag'in, you mus' er hu't yerse'f somehow er udder so you better lay still twel I kin git somebody ter he'p me cyar you 'way fum yer."

"Oh, I remember now, — the battle. We won, didn't we? The battle, Pete — the battle — is not lost!"

"You suttinly is got a good reckerlection. I ain' 'memberin' nuttin' 'tall 'bout losin' no battles," said Pete gruffly, to hide his feeling. "I's t'inkin' 'bout you, Marse Jasper, en how I kin get you 'way fum yer fo' dem Yankees teks you pris'ner."

"Where is Lieutenant Phillips? I thought I heard him call your Miss Catherine's name. Was I dreaming or was it his spirit. He is not dead, Pete, is he?"

"Who? Marse Garnett daid? Lor, nor, suh! Marse Garnett ain' so easy ter git kilt. *He's gone 'long down de road wid de yudders.*"

Pete laughed to carry out the deceit, but turned his head away.

"Fus' time, I s'pec', dat I eber tole a lie in my life, but dar's some lies dat de good Lawd don' write 'g'inst yo' name ner strek you daid fer, needer, I reckon, lak He did Marse Ananias, en dis is one er' 'em," he said to himself.

"I was sure, Pete, that your Marse Garnett was beside me when I heard your bugle."

"You cyan' be sho' er nuttin' in dis worl', Marse Jasper. 'Scuse me now; I's gwine git a man up in de woods dar ter he'p me cyar you back fo' dese yer Yanks kotches you en me bofe en puts us in prison en we ain' got no time to be projeckin.' I knows whar de man is en I's gwine fer 'im; he wuz driv outn his house by de firin'. He ain' no Yankee. He's what dey call a copperas haid."

Pete was soon back with his assistant. Carefully as they lifted Jasper, he sank again into merciful unconsciousness and knew not when he was taken across the death-red valley.

When they reached the hill on the other side of the field consciousness came back to Jasper, and with it a twinge of pain which brought a groan from the lips that were set with grim fierceness in the effort to suppress all sign of suffering.

"Easy, boys, easy," said a low, deep voice in a tone so gentle that the sound of it soothed away a part of the misery of the undressed wound stiffening in the burning heat of the path that skirted the battlefield. "Carry him gently for his pain and for the memory of the brave fellows we leave behind us."

Jasper lifted his heavy eyelids slowly and looked up to see what wondrous face might belong with this voice that was like a strain of half-forgotten music drifting around him in a dream which was otherwise only darkness and fear. There was a familiar note in the voice as if it might have fallen upon his ear often in the past when life was full in his veins and meant so much more than it could ever mean again.

The pain-worn face was so filled with tenderness that it brought tears to his eyes only to look at it, — tears that took away half his suffering in their flow but filled his heart with a deeper, wider pain, — a sense of loss that seemed world-wide.

The face into which Jasper looked was the same he had seen when the morning light made a dim radiance under the canopy of the trees brilliant with the greenery of summer, — the face at sight of which the men who dared not lift their voices in the ringing cheers that welled up in their hearts had raised their caps and bowed their heads in reverence and love,—the same face, yet not the same, for the battle ardor had died out and left it pale with the sorrow of a great loss, — perhaps the greatest loss that had ever come to a man since the first battle for supremacy was fought in a wildly ambitious world. For over each dead form that lay on that blood-crimsoned field his heart mourned as a father-heart mourns over the grave of a son. The tiger-eyes that had flamed with the fire of the coming conflict were softened in a gray tender light sadder than tears.

"Courage, my lad; we shall soon be among friends whose hearts and hands will bring you comfort."

The leader of the few who had in so short a time traveled the road to immortality and returned to earthly living looked back along the way.

"Far better for us," he said, stretching out his arms toward the long windrows left by the reaper Death, "had we stayed with them. But if *I* can cross that valley and live, cannot you?"

Thus the brave, tender-hearted General Pickett after the battle stood beside one of his "boys" as the sun sank behind the hills to rise again in golden glory when the night should pass.

The sun that had gilded the Flag of the Southern Cross had set to rise no more forever.

CHAPTER XIV

HOW THE NEWS CAME HOME

CATHERINE stood in the oak-paneled dining-hall and looked from the open window across to the servants' quarters. In the center of the wide space in front a dusky group had gathered. The night was murky and the scene was lit by pine-knot torches held in the hands of some half-grown youths whose faces, upturned to the flaring light, seemed to catch a demoniac glow that wavered and changed with the flickering glare. As the company moved about in the red light one might have fancied that a group from subterranean regions had met for spectral revelry.

Kate was thinking only how good and faithful they had been, — these black people of Magnolia Lawn. Politically they had been free for half a year. Practically they had been free much longer than that, for had they wished to leave the old plantation there had been nothing to prevent. It was their home and they loved it. What more could the wilderness of freedom offer them? Many of the neighboring servants had chosen the uncertainties of that great unknown country rather than the safety of the tried and known. She did not think it strange that they had done so. Though the offered gift bear nothing of freedom but its name, it yet holds out to the imagination such brilliant possibilities that only a great love can outshine it in glory. Such a love these faithful hearts held for the old home and its inmates.

There was a barbaric splendor in the scene that carried Kate's fancy into the fantastic shadows of oriental traditions.

The negroes had formed a semicircle around the illumined space and the light flickering over their faces gave them an unearthly expression of awesome enchantment.

An old man who formed the keystone of the arch began to sing slowly in a deep melancholy tone a song commemorative of the manifold virtues and sorrowful fate of one "Poor Uncle Ned," who had lived a long time ago and had gone to a rest well earned by a protracted life of good deeds and self-sacrifice. He had apparently been forced to relinquish most of the attractions which earthly existence offers to the average human being.

His fingers wuz long lak de cane in de brake
En he had no eyes fer ter see;
En he had no teefs fet ter eat de corn-cake,
So he had ter let de corn-cake be.

All joined in the chorus, which welled up in a heavy surge of woe:

Den hang up de fiddle en de bow-o-o-o,
Lay down de shubble en de hoe-o-o-o;
Fer dar's no mo' wu'k fer po' ole Ned,
He's gone whar de good niggers go."

As the first note of the chorus swelled out in a volume of sad melody a girl glided into the center of the circle and began a slow, weird, mystic dance, swaying backward and forward and from side to side, keeping time with her sinuous movements to the rise and fall of the dirge. To them the life and death of the good old black man of whom they sang who had "died long ago, long ago" and who "had no wool on de top er his haid in de place whar de wool ought ter grow," were as real and as new as were the scenes of their every-day life.

When the funeral ode was ended the same deep rich voices rang out in a merry song with a chorus of laughter after each stanza. A half-grown boy ran into the circle and began a clog-dance to the gay notes of the banjo and the clank of the bones, followed by another and yet another, all joining in heartily with the laughing chorus to which their twinkling feet kept time.

"What children they are," thought Kate, as she joined in the laugh. "They weep over imaginary sorrows and laugh over fancied joys without a thought of the realities of life. Ah, here comes Uncle Zeke. Why are you not having fun down at the cabins with the others? Dear me, what has happened to please you so?"

"Happened! Miss Kate, why sumpn's happened ter mek yo' Ung Zeke want ter do mo' dan dance. He wants ter shout lak he'd jes' got 'ligion fer de fus' time."

"What is it, Uncle Zeke? Do tell me."

"Well, Miss Kate, Marse Carey's jes' come fum Richmon' en brung de news dat 'way up dar at de Norf what Marse Gen'l Lee's been a foughtin', dat we-all's whopped dem Yankees en dat we-all's army's marchin' ter Wash'ton en dat we-all 'ill be dar termorrer er de naix' day sho'. Oh, de Jubilee am a comin', Miss Kate, it am a comin'!"

"Are you sure, Uncle Zeke?" she cried, her cheeks aglow and her eyes dancing.

"Sho' en sartin! Miss Kate, sho', fer Marse Carey jes' dis minute got back fum Richmon' whar dey knows ebbyt'ing, en dat's what dey tole him. De news come dar yis'day en has jes' got 'roun' to us."

Victory! For one instant Kate's heart stood still as if it would never beat again. The world was dark before her and she heard strange sounds far off on an unknown shore. Something seemed to grasp at her throat and she could not breathe. Intense joy had brought a helpless pain like that which comes with intense grief. Then light came back. Tears filled her eyes, — the tears that lie alike at the heart of a great happiness and a great sorrow. Her cheeks, which had gone suddenly pale with the shock of joy, blossomed out redder than the roses that bloomed in Omar's garden. The triumph in her heart flamed into her eyes and dried away the tears.

Her first thought was of Jasper. The war was ended and he would soon come home, — come home to her! The long terror of battle was over and sweet peace had come at last. For what could there be more to do than to go to Washington and offer to withdraw the army from Northern soil on condition that the South should own herself and live her own life? What a magnificent, glorious life it would be with their wide fertile lands, their beautiful homes, the power to make their own laws adapted to their own needs.

But what were laws and national interests to Kate? Jasper was coming home. What wider meaning than that had peace for her?

And Garnett, — yes, he would come, too. In the first rush of joy she had not thought of him. She would be glad to see him, though. He was a dear fellow and had been good to Jasper. That either would not come had never dawned upon her thought. Lovers and cousins and fathers and brothers had been left on the field, and sweethearts and cousins and sisters and daughters had walked black-robed in the sun, and the darkness of their sorrow had dimmed the light of day for her. That she should suffer like loss had never come within the range of her imaginings. The field-glass of youth sees no cloud on the horizon of the future even when the eyes of youth are forced to recognize a present darkness.

In the exuberance of his feeling Uncle Zeke

executed a pigeon-wing with a lightsomeness not to be surpassed by the gayest youth in the quarters.

"Bravo, Uncle Zeke! Bravo! But why are you celebrating a victory for the South? The North is fighting your battle. The Northern President has set you free."

"Ef he did I didn' neber go, did I?"

"No; but if General Lee's army goes to Washington it might happen that you would lose your opportunity to go. I suppose the yoke is heavy in proportion to the remoteness of the possibility of shaking it off."

"I don' know nuttin' 'tall 'bout no 'moteness, but dar wan't neber no heaby yoke 'roun' my naik, Miss Kate. I cyan' say how 'tis wid ole Marser. I reckon he's had de yoke 'roun' his naik all his natchul born life but he don' neber say much, dough I did hyer him say oncet dat ef we-all didn' run away moughty soon he'd jes *hab* ter do it. But eben he neber done it. He wuz jes' projickin' wid we-alls en skeerin' us kaze he wuz mad 'bout Dick lettin' de ca'ige run 'way wid de hosses; den ole Jake tuck de feber en Jim en Pete fit a fought 'bout Jemima Ann, en all dat meked ole Marse kinder discouraged, I reckon, en so he up en th'eatened we-all. But, lor, Miss Kate, I ain' skeert ole Marser gwineter run 'way en leabe we-all en one t'ing sho', we-all ain' *neber gwineter run 'way en leabe him*, en we don' want him eber ter 'sult us a gibin' us no 'mansumashum papers, needer, fer we-all cyan' do 'dout one anudder."

Kate looked over to where the clog dancer was keeping vigorous time to the orchestra of banjo, bones, clapping hands, and musical voices.

"Have you told them about the great news?"

"Nor'm. Whut's de use? Dem niggers is happy ez long ez dey's dancin' en a singin' en hit don' mek no diffunce whut dey's dancin' 'bout, nuther. Hit mought ez well be 'bout a possum en a sweet 'tater ez 'bout a flag en a kentry fer all dey'd keer, sepn dey'd t'ink a possum en a sweet 'tater wuz wuf mo' ter fight 'bout. Dey'll know it ez soon ez ole Marse comes, anyhow. He's ober at Marse Carey's en hyeard it 'fo' I hyeard it. En lis'n — lis'n — lis'n, Miss Kate! Lis'n ter dat bell! Don' you hyer it sayin', 'Vic'try! Vic'try! Vic'try! De Souf's free! De Souf's free!' Did you eber hyer any shoutin' soun' sweeter, er singin', eeder, ez ter dat, dan de music dem bells is a ringin' out ter tell us dat de Lawd en His angels is done en perwailed en dat de Souf's a free eberlastin' libin' glory ter de name er de Lawd or Gawd fereber mo'!"

The old man lifted his clasped hands and looked upward with an expression of beatific happiness illuminating his face.

At that moment Kate saw a sable youth leap the fence and run toward the quarters, shouting some message the words of which she could not distinguish.

Each reveler paused instantly in the attitude in which he chanced to be. The clog dancer stood on one foot, the other held in air as if executing the next step. Kate observed how graceful his lithe figure was in that pose. Old Cæsar's bow was lifted in preparation for beginning a spirited and dashing strain. The bones held by Thomas Jefferson Monroe remained crossed at the exact musical angle. George Washington Bonaparte's hand was arrested on its downward flight toward the last note of "Juba dis en Juba dat, en Juba 'roun' de kittle er fat." Kate thought of the city that fell mute when the Sleeping Beauty sank into her long slumber.

The reaction came. Every figure bounded into activity. The music rang out with a wild note of triumph that filled the night. The bones rattled out their victorious message as if the joyful news had brought life again to them and clothed them with sentient flesh and given them a heart to thrill with triumph. The clapping of hands resounded uproariously. A chorus of voices rolled out in a jubilee and the wave of melody widened out over a sea that had no shore.

"Dey sho' is got dar Ferginia blood het up," said Zeke with admiration. "'Pear lak w'edder dey's fiel' hands er bodyguards dese niggers is all got heart feelin's fer we-all's cause."

Through the wild uproar of the plantation surged the solemn, proud, triumphant yet almost melancholy refrain of the bells, "The South is free! The South is free!"

Thus the news came home. Far-off nations learned the fateful decision of that great conflict before accurate tidings of it could percolate through the stone wall which war had built around the South. Rumor was optimistic, and the hope of a great victory swelled under her cheerful ministrations. For a little moment, the South felt the bliss of triumph.

Then darkness fell.

CHAPTER XV

THE RETURN TO BRIGHTVIEW

"PRAISE de Lawd! We's gittin' to'a'ds home, Marse Jasper. Yas, suh, we's jis' sightin' de ole Slocum place now. Praise de Lawd! We's mos' dar at las'."

Jasper Carrington lay half asleep on an army cot in the old covered wagon in which his faithful servant was taking his wounded master home. The negro, waving a fan gently to and fro over the white face, glanced at Jasper's cap under the driver's seat. It had served as a fan until a thoughtful woman at the last stopping place had given them the palm-leaf. The gray cloth was faded and dusty, the gold cord tarnished and frayed. He took it up and turned it over. In the crown was a strip of white silk, discolored now, on which was embroidered the owner's name. The old man could not read, but he knew the meaning of the mysterious characters and that they were the work of Kate's dainty fingers.

Colonel Carrington moved restlessly.

"Have we passed the road to Magnolia Lawn yet, Pete?"

"No, suh; but we's comin' to it; we's jamby dar."

The old man looked wistfully at his master.

"'Pear lak ter me, Marse Jasper, dat when we does come ter it we'd better turn in dar. Miss Kate ain' neber gwine fergib we-alls ef we don' stop en pay 'em a visit."

"Yes, but I can't stop like this, Pete; no, not like this. You do as I tell you and go on to Brightview." The voice, though weary, had an unmistakable element of firmness. "And, remember, Pete, if we meet any one on the road, not one word, and don't you even dare show your black face. We are just a team passing through the country, that's all. You understand?"

"Yas, Marse Jasper. I understan's."

"And you promise me, Pete?"

The old man groaned inwardly.

"Yas, suh; I promises you all ret. De Lawd ha' mussy!"

Every foot of the way was familiar to Uncle Pete. He peered eagerly ahead past the driver's portly figure and saw two or three children in the bushes by the roadside. Only members of the household of Magnolia Lawn would be gathering berries on that stretch of road, miles away from any other habitation. His old heart gave a jump and with difficulty he suppressed a cry. It was a chance — a slim chance — but the only one, and he would take it.

He ceased fanning and closely watched the sleeper, who did not stir. As the wagon neared the children Pete crept cautiously forward and picked up the gray cap. Then he took the large white handkerchief with which he had been wiping away the drops that occasionally broke out on the young man's face, threw it over his head and leaned across the seat.

The children stood up, dumb, stolid, to watch the wagon go by. They did not move even when a man's cap, hurled by a long arm from the front of the cart, fell at the feet of the largest boy. A few moments later Pete, whose face was still masked, watching them from the rear of the cart, saw them pick up the cap, examine it with great excitement and shrill little cries, and then set off with it at full speed up the lane to Magnolia Lawn.

There remained still a weary three hours' drive. Colonel Carrington slept fitfully and as they neared Brightview restlessly insisted on sitting up.

"We are almost there, Pete. Another turn; — there, driver, go in at this first gate."

"Lawd ha' mussy, look! Is dat we-all's home? Is dat Brightview? Dat cyan't be we-all's home, sho'; bu'nt up lak dat!"

Pete's bent frame straightened up and over his face spread a peculiar pallor. His master, too, went even whiter than before. Neither spoke as the wagon bumped heavily over the ill-kept road.

Beyond the burned trees stood the blackened frame, the charred timbers of the old house — one wing only standing, the remaining two-thirds of the structure leveled almost to the ground.

Colonel Carrington laid a hand affectionately on the wrinkled black one clinched on the side of the cot.

"It is still home, Pete, as long as there is a stone left, — still home."

Pete turned pathetic eyes on his master's face.

"Ole Mistis? Miss Ca'line?" He barely whispered the words.

"I hope they have not heard," was the reply. "When I left they went to my cousin's in Nansemond."

"We-all mus' do a heap er mendin' en fixin' up den 'fo' dey gits back ag'in. Ole Pete allus wuz good at carpent'in' wuk. I hope dem Yankees lef' de tools in de tool house." Then after a pause, "You jes' herry up en git well, Marse Jasper, en you en de ole man gwine hab some fun projeckin' 'roun' en buildin' de ole place up ag'in fer somebody!"

The wing that remained contained but three rooms — the long, low sitting-room of hallowed memories, and two small chambers above. This part had been saved by the brave efforts of the loyal servants who had risked their lives to put out the flames when the destroyers had gone.

Some of the old Brightview servants came out with faces keen with curiosity which suddenly changed to alarm when they saw their master lying helpless on the cot, then to delight when he called their names in a cheerful voice and assured them that he was not much hurt.

Colonel Carrington was carried slowly into the sitting-room and the cot put down gently near the west window where there was a faint breeze stirring. Here the desolation, the tragedy, seemed more awful still. Apparently the vandal sword had been ruthlessly swept to right and left in an attempt to destroy what could not be carried away.

The old cook had hurried off to get fresh milk and eggs for her "Marser," joyous in the thought of having one of her "w'ite folks" again to serve.

Jasper lay and looked about him, an occasional groan escaping his lips. Troops of olden memories had followed him through the doorway and were gathering around his cot,—memories of olden home-comings when the old house stood stately and fair and gave him sweet welcome that gladdened his heart. He remembered the last time he had come home, when mother and sister had met him with loving caresses and the one girl in all the world had taken a wild night ride to warn him of danger.

Old Pete bustled about, making a great deal of fuss over getting things comfortable, for it would never do to let the young master see that he, too, could have laid himself down and groaned in anguish of spirit.

Presently, after he had been given some hot milk, he called out wistfully:

"I thought I heard horses, Pete. I wish I could see the road from here. Oh, it would be so good to catch a glimpse of some of the home people, wouldn't it?"

"I ain' hyeared no hosses ner nuthin', Marse Jasper. I reckon it's de team gwine back. I spec', too, dat fool driver is skeert er be bein' cotched on dese onfamilous roads atter dark. En hit's gwine ter be dark, too, in th'ee er fo' hours fum now."

Suddenly for a second there appeared in the doorway a girlish figure in a riding habit. Finger on lip, the other hand beckoning, the girl receded into the shadows. Pete nodded and then went to Jasper's side. The young man lay looking out of the window.

"You lemme raise you jes' a mite, Marse Jasper, ter ease you while I rummage 'roun' ter see ef dere's anythin' lef' in de house ter mek we-all mo' comf'ble. Dis yer do's got ter be kep' shet 'count er de win'. You gits 'nuf a'r fum all dem winders 'dout habin' de do' wide open, too."

He went out and drew the door to behind him.

Kate and her father stood on the veranda, the girl nervously plaiting into folds the soft felt hat she had worn. Uncle Zeke was in the shadows beyond, at his feet a big basket and a bundle of bedding.

"So you have brought your young master home, Uncle Pete. I hope he is not badly wounded," said the Colonel.

"Is he much hurt? He isn't going to die, is he, Uncle Pete?"

"Lor, no, Honey. Don' you werry none, Miss Kate. Marse Jasper jes' shot in de laig wid one er dem big bullets en peppered up some wid de li'le ones, dat's all. Ole Pete gwine hab 'im walkin' 'roun' en dancin' 'fo' de een er de week."

"Really, Uncle Pete? You wouldn't deceive me, would you?"

"No'm; hones' ter gracious, Miss Kate, dat I wouldn'. Don' you s'pose Ole Pete'd be skeert, too, ef dar wuz anythin' ter be skeert 'bout?"

"I must see him this minute. I can't wait. I won't startle him."

"No'm, you cyan' startleize Marse Jasper, but ef I tole him you wuz hyer he'd fergit all 'bout dem game laigs en git offn dat cot 'fo' ole Pete could stop him, en dat wouldn' neber do."

"Well, you go in and keep him from getting up and father and I will just come in slowly and let him see us."

The old man turned as he was about to open the door and said:

"You better let yo' pa stay outside, Honey, en come in by yo'se'f firs'."

Uncle Pete entered the sitting-room.

"Did you find anything, Pete? Oh, I wish I could get up."

"Did I find anything? Well, you'll see in a minute what I found, Marse Jasper. Jes' wait en you'll see what I foun'."

The old man chuckled as he spread over Jasper, with an almost womanly touch, a lavender-scented sheet from a chest saved by the servants from the flames. Then he went around to the other side of the cot and stood before him, shutting out the view of the door.

"You don' want no mo' milk, does you, Marse Jasper?"

"No; what's that? I thought I heard a footstep."

The sick man started; Uncle Pete moved away.

"Kate! Kate! My darling; — my darling, am I dreaming?"

"No, suh, Marse Jasper, you ain't dreamin'; bress yo' heart. *Now you knows whut de ole man foun'.*"

Out of the shadow she came into the golden radiance that shone from the west. Her face was white with tense emotion and her dark eyes were aglow. The wondrous picture held him motionless and silent as the realization of her presence dawned upon him. She came into the sunset glory and knelt beside the cot. His arms were around her and his lips in the wind-blown tangle of her hair.

Pete tiptoed out, a suspicious moisture in his eyes.

"Kate, my sweetheart, my love! How did you know? How did you come here? Little girl, little girl, don't cry so. I'm all right — all right."

The wonder of it all filled his heart again and he said: — "How did you know?"

"One of the boys brought me a cap with the very strip of silk on which I had embroidered your name, saying that it had been thrown from a wagon that went down the lane, by a negro with something white over his face. He said that there was a dead soldier lying in the wagon. I knew that Uncle Pete had brought you home and we came at once."

"That old rascal, Pete!" said Jasper, with a smile of content.

Half an hour later Pete tiptoed back. Kate sat in the window, her eyes shining. Jasper held her hands and his gaze did not leave her face.

"You must tell me what you need, Uncle Pete," said Kate; "everything you haven't got, and you shall have it the first thing in the morning. Or to-night, if need be. Uncle Zeke and I must be going in a few minutes. Father will remain with Jasper, dear heart. I shall be back in the morning and bring Doctor Gorham, just to make sure."

"I sont fer de Doctor de firs' t'ing, en I's 'spectin' him any minute."

"You are so thoughtful, Uncle Pete, and just to think of your bringing him home by yourself. Where is my Cousin Garnett? But I suppose he couldn't get leave. Your master tells me you saw him last going down the road."

"Yas'm; *he wuz gwine down de road.*" Uncle Zeke's throat tightened. "Dat's how I seed him, Honey. *Gwine down de road 'long wid de yudders* — happy lak en smilin'; smilin' jes' lak he allus done." He went on hastily to cover the confusion of his mistake. "De Gen'l he holp me a heap en he tol' me ter fotch Marse Jasper 'long home en I fotch him. 'Here's de money fer yo' suspenses, Pete,' he say, 'ca'y him easy, en git all de holp you needs.'"

A glow of love and reverence lit Jasper's eyes as he said:

"That is our General's loving spirit, always around us to aid and bless. You can never know what General Pickett has been to me; — a strong arm to support, a steady hand to guide, a wise head to counsel, a gentle heart to sympathize in joy and sorrow. An inspiration on march and field, he is a living force to give his men the power to endure and achieve. The hottest place in the battle is where he is seen leading his Division, and there is not a man of us who would not proudly follow him to death."

Kate pressed his hand, silent with the deep feeling that surged through her heart. Then she turned to the window.

"I must go now; the sun has set," she said softly. "But not for us; nor for the South. For all of us a grand, a glorious, sunrise, and a perfect day, Jasper, dear."

"Yes, sweetheart mine. A new home, a new South, but the old, old love."

The gray dusk closed about them. Pete had crept away into the shadows and through the twilight came the clear sweet sound of Kate's bugle-call.